THE
WORK
RETREAT

JE ROWNEY

LITTLE FOX
PUBLISHING

Also by JE Rowney

I Can't Sleep
The Woman in the Woods
Other People's Lives
The Book Swap
Gaslight
The House Sitter

For further information and to receive a free book, please visit the author's website.

http://jerowney.com/about-je-rowney

Disclaimer:
This is a work of fiction. All characters, places and businesses within this novel are works of fiction and are not based on, or representative of, real world persons, places, or organisations.

This book was formerly published under the title "Zero Days Since Last Incident"

PROLOGUE

Jonathan Jackson looked down at the man dangling from the ledge. Wide brown eyes stared back; a panicked plea came almost breathlessly from the younger man's chapped lips.

"Pull me up, mate."

The words took so much effort to force from Thompson's mouth that they were almost inaudible.

But Jackson heard.

The wind that had been building all day was whipping against Jackson's face. He wanted shelter. He wanted warmth. He wanted to be back at home. He could turn and walk away. No one would ever know that he had found Mark, let alone what had happened next. Mark Thompson had brought this upon himself. Not just by leaving the group, heading out on his own, trying to be the hero, not that. Mark was not his colleague; he was his enemy - and that had been Mark's own choice.

"Jackson," Mark gasped. "Please."

Jackson could feel the throbbing in his eye socket where the other man had landed a lucky blow. A slow, steady trickle of blood coursed past the side of his eye, down his cheek. He could tell the others it had been a stray branch, an accident. No need for them to know it was Mark. No need to…

"Jackson!" A woman's voice from the edge of the clearing. "What the hell is going on?"

ONE

It was a standard Thursday. Meetings, phone calls, emails in and out. Jonathan Jackson was working on one of the company's most important client proposals. The Tursten Mitchell account had the potential to put InnovaTech on the map – and Jackson was at the wheel.

After months of research, analysis, and tireless discussion with the Tursten Mitchell bigwigs, Jackson was nearing the deadline to send the proposal.

Fifty-two years old. Not in bad shape. He still had his hair. He had been handsome once.

With over a decade spent at InnovaTech, he had been one of the first to join Thornicroft. He had believed in the company and its mission statement when no one else had. Richard Thornicroft wanted the best. Best sales team, best analysts, best support services. InnovaTech was about people – or at least that was the dream. Jackson had recognised the opportunity as a chance to shine, a chance to be something. Over a decade spent waiting to realise that dream. The wait was almost over.

The email was drafted, the hard work completed.

Let it settle. Grab a drink. Come back with fresh eyes and check it over before hitting the button.

Jackson clicked his mouse to lock the screen, got up from his chair and walked with unusual light-headedness into the staff kitchen.

Was the culmination of six months' work really giving him the same butterflies in his stomach that he had only experienced before when he married Helena?

Now he was on the verge of sealing the deal with Tursten Mitchell, he might at last be able to cut back on the overtime, the late nights at the office away from his wife.

He smiled to himself as he set his bottle on the kitchen counter.

Everything was finally coming together.

Across the room, Mark Thompson was sitting at the dining table, a half-eaten sandwich in one hand

and a tablet in the other. Jackson knew Thompson had been there a while from the smell of coffee and the empty drip machine.

Jackson shook his head in bemusement and exasperation. Mark's focus on food and drink seemed out of touch with work demands. How did he manage to stay slim while eating junk?

In Jackson's eyes, Mark was wasting time, lost in the flavours of his lunch, while the fast-paced world of technology development moved on without him. Mark was younger, and better qualified, but he lacked the acumen and experience that had led to Jackson being chosen as the lead for the Tursten Mitchell account.

Too late, Jackson realised that he had made eye contact with his colleague, and Mark stood, leaping over to his side.

"Whatcha got there, buddy? A margarita?" Thompson prodded at Jackson's drink shaker.

Jackson gave Mark a silent look of disdain.

Undeterred, Thompson grabbed the plastic container off the counter and turned it over to read the label.

"What's this? Magic Build?" Thompson stepped back dramatically and raised his hands in an act of faux submission, the protein mix held high. "If you're building your magic, I don't want to get in your way."

Whoever said "hell is other people" probably worked in an office like InnovaTech.

"Just put it down," Jackson said with the hint of a sigh.

"You gonna cast a spell on me if I don't?"

"Hilarious, Thompson," Jackson said, placing his shaker on the counter and reaching out for the tub that Mark was still holding onto. "Now give it back."

"Okay, okay," Mark said as Jackson swiped towards him.

He didn't let go of the tub. Instead, as Jackson moved forward, he took a step away, moving the mix away from him.

"Calm down, friend," Mark smiled.

Jackson made another pass at his mix, and Mark carried on the game.

"Fine," Jackson said with a forced calmness. "I don't have time for this."

Mark's expression soured, and he put Jackson's shaker down with a reluctant grunt. It was pointless holding it up since Jackson had lost interest in the battle.

"Oh yes," he said, as though just remembering something. "The Tursten Mitchell report. How's that coming on, buddy? Big day today. Got everything ready to go? Dotted those Ts and crossed those Is?"

Mark laughed at his own joke, but Jackson didn't respond.

"I'm fine," Jackson said, controlling the terse tone in his voice the best he could manage.

It was the big one. This was his most critical contract, and everything had to be impeccable. This contract could be career-changing. Twelve years working in the same job role, with idiots like Thompson coming in and climbing the ranks as he patiently waited his turn.

"Thank you," Jackson added, with a professional smile.

He tentatively reached for his protein, testing whether Mark was going to pull it away again, and when Thompson remained still, Jackson scooped it up and kept a firm hold. No point putting it back in the cupboard. He would take it to his desk, keep it in his drawer where his oh-so-funny colleague couldn't get his hands on it.

"You know where I am," Mark said, "if you need me."

"I know where you are."

Jackson took a swig of the shake and held back his grimace. He hadn't mixed it enough; the powdery texture almost made him gag, but he had to keep a straight face as he walked past his coworker and back into the office.

TWO

Mark Thompson observed Jonathan Jackson, his elder but not his superior, as they sat across from each other in the InnovaTech office.

Tursten Mitchell should have been Mark Thompson's client. Technically, Jackson was the more experienced of the two, but Thompson had a track record of successfully scoring two of the most important clients that the company had onboarded over the past year. Plus, Thompson knew how to use buzzwords like "*onboarded*" that made old-school Jackson screw his nose up. Not that he would say anything, though. Jackson sat quietly, kept the peace, walked the line. Jackson was a good guy, and as far as Thompson was concerned, good guys deserved to finish last.

Mark Bradley Thompson. First class degree from King's College. Six years of post-grad experience in West Force before being headhunted by Richard Thornicroft himself to take this job at InnovaTech. He was the one that should have been chosen to head the Tursten Mitchell account. Instead, Thornicroft had passed him over for Jackson. Jackson, who had achieved little more than dragging along in Mark's slipstream for the past three years. It was ridiculous. Jonathan Jackson. Some crappy degree from somewhere. One of the few team members that had been with Thornicroft and InnovaTech since its inception.

Thornicroft was giving him his chance to shine. That must be it.

The look of concentration on Jackson's face was so intense that Thompson almost broke out into laughter. His brow furrowed; his eyes pierced the screen.

"Have you sent it yet?"

Mark feigned friendly indifference as he called across the desk.

Jackson didn't look up from the screen. His fingers were tapping on his keyboard as he made frantic adjustments to the Tursten Mitchell contract. There was no time for conversation, no leeway for chat. Securing this deal would elevate InnovaTech to new heights of success and recognition in their industry. It was a game-changer, and Jackson had been selected as MVP.

Mark's eyes remained on his coworker. Were those beads of perspiration that he saw on Jackson's temple? Jackson was going to crack under the pressure, Mark could already tell. Why the older man had been chosen to lead on this project was beyond Mark's comprehension. He had the better track record. He had delivered the Bell contract. He had gathered the leads that had brought Tursten Mitchell to InnovaTech's virtual door. He should have been the one to deliver.

"I can give you a hand if you need it, mate. I know this is the big one for you," he offered. "Want me to check it over before you…"

Mark pulled himself out of his swivel chair and walked around the desk space to stand behind his older colleague.

"I'm fine, Mark. Really." Jackson breathed steadily. "Thank you."

Mark leaned in closer, as though it was difficult to see the words on the screen from where he was standing. Jackson felt the weight of his colleague press against the back of his chair, his breath against the side of his face. Fighting the urge to lash out, Jackson braced himself and remained calm.

"This figure here," Mark jabbed a thick finger at the screen. "Is that correct?"

Jackson pushed back on his chair slightly, just enough to judder Mark backwards.

"It's all correct," Jackson said, his voice flat and even. "I'm going to send the email now, so there's no need for you to worry about me and my contract anymore."

"Our contract," Mark said tersely.

"But I…"

"Ours. InnovaTech's," Mark expanded, with smug satisfaction. "This contract means a lot to the entire company, Jacko."

"Jackson," Jackson said. "Or Jonathan. Jon, even. Not Jacko. Never Jacko, okay?"

Mark laughed softly and stood down.

"Sure, Jonnie. No problem at all. I was…"

Jackson read through the email that would accompany the briefing paper one final time. Everything was perfect. He knew it would be. He knew he had made a flawless submission for Tursten Mitchell. There was no way that they could choose another company over InnovaTech when they saw what was on offer, and the prices that Jackson had presented to them. InnovaTech wasn't the most well known in the business yet, not even locally, but they were the best. And Jackson was the best of the best.

No matter what Mark thought.

Thompson stood barely a foot behind Jon, watching studiously as he read. The email was concise and effective, he couldn't disagree with that. There was only one thing missing. Jackson hadn't added the attachment.

Mark flicked his eyes up to the clock. It was only a few minutes before five, the submission deadline. If Jackson didn't pull the trigger soon, he was going to piss off a lot of suits, starting with Richard Thornicroft, the head of InnovaTech. More importantly, if the documents weren't sent in time, there was no way InnovaTech would win the contract. Jackson's ass would be on the line, hell he might even be fired for such a mistake.

No more Jonathan Jackson.

No more competition from across the desk.

"Looks great," Mark said, trying to sound as though he was actually impressed by Jon's attempt. "Nearly time." He pointed up at the clock.

Jackson batted him away, with the impatience of a father constantly bothered by a petulant toddler.

"Yes, Mark. Thank you."

"Three minutes," Mark persisted.

"Okay," Jackson snapped, finally giving in to the tension that had been building. He clicked the send button and closed the email client.

"Yes!" Mark yelped. He patted Jackson firmly on the shoulder. "Well done, mate. Well done."

The email had gone. The response from the client wouldn't come through until at least the next day, and Mark knew exactly what it would say.

No go, Jacko.

You fudged it.

The biggest contract that InnovaTech never

had, and all thanks to Jonnie Jackson.

"Thanks," Jackson said. Mark's joyful reaction to the contract being submitted was more than he had expected, but then again, the contract was more than he had expected too. He had worked his entire career to get to that point. All the hours he had put in. The overtime, the evenings apart from his kind, patient, understanding wife, Helena. Finally, everything was about to pay off for him.

"Thanks, man," he said again.

Mark grinned and ruffled Jackson's hair. Jackson smiled and let him.

THREE

Performance review period was the bane of Sarah Collins's existence. Every year, she sent out reminders for the staff to complete their online forms, and every year, the lazy desk slaves failed to meet the deadline. It didn't help that her assistant had taken her full entitlement of maternity leave. How was everything made so easy for people now?

Sarah had barely clicked send on the final warning email when there was a knock on her door. Human resources was one of the few departments that had their own office, and as her assistant was on leave, the office was basically hers.

"Who is it?" the redhead called, not moving from her desk.

"Emily Shawcross," a small voice sounded through the door.

Sarah let out a sigh and looked at the clock on the corner of her computer screen. 16:55. Five minutes until she was officially off the clock. She would give the intern that long, and not a minute more.

"Okay," she said.

"Can I come in?" Emily's voice was tentative.

"Okay," Sarah repeated, more loudly.

The door opened and the carefully put-together intern stepped inside. She looked as though she had Googled office-appropriate clothing and chosen the most personality-stripping outfit she could find. Bland white shirt, knee-length pencil skirt and shoes that would suit Sarah's grandmother. If Sarah had that kind of figure instead of the fast-food-addiction curves she had developed over the years, she would definitely have put together a more fetching wardrobe.

"I don't have long," Sarah said, looking at the clock again. Two minutes had already ticked by.

"Oh," Emily said. "I won't take up much of your time." She walked closer to the HR manager's desk but stopped short of sitting in the chair opposite her. Sarah didn't invite her to sit, so she stood awkwardly behind it.

"What is it?" Sarah sighed, turning her eyes

from the screen.

Emily took a visible breath and opened her mouth to speak.

"It's not the best time," Sarah interrupted. "I have to get all these performance reviews ticked off before the end of the week."

"I'm sorry," Emily squeaked. "I could come back another time."

"You're here now. I've already had to stop what I'm doing. Let's get this over with."

The young intern nodded in understanding, and then spoke. Her words came out in a rapid, nervy torrent. "I just wanted to discuss my future here at InnovaTech. I've really enjoyed my time as an intern, and I was hoping there might be opportunities for a permanent position."

"Have you rehearsed that?" Sarah laughed.

"Um. Yes," Emily's face reddened, and she tried to return a smile.

Sarah cut her laughter, keen not to give the wrong impression, and Emily's smile faded.

Sarah's eyes wandered back to her computer screen. Then, with an exasperated sigh, she answered. "A permanent position? Do you think you might be getting ahead of yourself?" she retorted, her words dripping with condescension. Before Emily responded, Sarah continued. "We don't usually hire interns for full-time roles here. I thought you'd been made aware of that."

Emily kept a straight face, trying to maintain

her composure. "I understand," she said. "But I've been working hard and I'm passionate about the work we do. I believe I can make valuable contributions to the team." Her voice trembled slightly.

Unimpressed, Sarah smirked.

"Passion can only get you so far, Emily. You're just an intern, and we have enough experienced professionals already." She paused and tapped at her keyboard, bringing up Emily's personnel record. Sarah nodded, as though confirming something she already knew. "If there were any openings, they'd go to someone with more qualifications," she asserted, her voice ice-cold.

Sarah could almost see Emily visibly deflate as she took in the words. Yet the young woman persisted.

"Is there any advice you can give me on how I can improve my chances for a future role? I really want to grow with this company," she asked. She was determined, Sarah would give her that.

Sarah leaned back in her chair, crossing her arms.

"Well, for starters, stop being so eager to move up the ladder. Focus on your internship for now and learn from the others. Then do something that stands out. Make yourself indispensable. But let's be realistic, Emily. There are no guarantees," she stated with cool bluntness. It was time to close the conversation down. She wanted to be out of the front door of the building before the clock made it to six. The best of the ready meals in the reductions section were always taken if you weren't first to the chiller when they started slapping the stickers on.

"Okay," Emily smiled again, as though Sarah had given her some good advice. "I will do that, thank you."

Focus on the internship. Keep learning. It was obvious, really, but with no guarantee of a future, it was all she could do. The enthusiasm that she had brought into the room with her had been replaced with disappointment and frustration, but there was still a glimmer of hope.

"Okay," Sarah said, tapping on her keyboard, to clarify that the unplanned meeting was over. Emily couldn't see that she had opened a web browser and was checking out a dress on eBay that she wanted to bid on.

"Thanks," Emily said again. She wasn't sure whether to call the HR manager Sarah or Ms Collins, so she decided on neither. With a heavy heart, she turned to the door and left her positivity behind her.

The seed of doubt had been firmly planted in Emily's mind about her future at InnovaTech. Would she ever be taken seriously or given a real chance to prove herself?

FOUR

Mark expected the bomb to drop overnight, and to arrive at the office to find the aftermath. Jackson was sitting at his desk already when Mark logged in, just before nine. There was a fresh coffee on his coaster, no doubt prepped for him by simpering Emily. His post was stacked neatly on his mouse mat. Everything looked the same as it had every other day that he had worked at InnovaTech. The same dull routine. The precise pattern of monotonous morning greetings and the same shitty view across the low divider between him and Jonathan Jackson.

"Any news?" he thought about asking and then changed his mind. Mark knew what the news was

going to be. If it had already landed, there was no way that Jackson would be sitting across from him, sipping his ridiculous hot water and lemon. If it had already landed, Jackson would most likely not be sitting across from him at all.

Instead of speaking, Thompson slumped in his chair and opened his schedule.

When he had left the previous evening, his calendar for the morning was blank, which left him time to work on his own client accounts. Now, there was a sneaky nine fifteen meeting, red flagged, nagging at him from his screen.

"Fu…" he spoke aloud and cut the word off before the expletive reached anybody's ears. Thornicroft had a zero-tolerance policy for what he described as *'uncouth language'* in the office.

"Keep it couth," Mark muttered to himself.

There was a note tagged on the appointment request.

Need to touch base ASAP. Minor hitch with the Agrana project. K.

K was Karen Atkins, software engineer, and the *minor hitch* was no doubt a lot more serious than she was letting on if she had the audacity to blindside him with a nine fifteen.

"Little b…" Mark checked himself again.

He looked over the desk divider at Jackson, who appeared engrossed in whatever he was working on, but still undisturbed. Perhaps he had realised his mistake the night before and somehow managed to send the proposal through to Tursten Mitchell. Could they possibly have high enough regard for Jackson to allow him to submit late?

"Can you stop that?" Jon said, without looking up.

"Hmm?" Mark said.

"That," Jackson pointed, still without raising his eyes.

Mark hadn't even realised that he had been tapping his pen on the desk in a staccato rhythm.

"Right, uh, yeah."

His mind was elsewhere, and it wasn't on whatever Atkins wanted to drop on his doorstep. He wanted to be present when Jackson got word of his mistakes. Everything else could wait.

He started to write an email to the software engineer to cancel the meeting.

No can do. Busy all morning. Touch base later.

Without suggesting an alternative meeting time, Mark clicked send and let the bad news wind its way across the room to where he could see the back of Karen's blonde curls flattened against her chair. From behind, she almost looked attractive.

Mark smirked to himself, and took a long sip from his coffee, before instantly spluttering it out, showering his screen.

"Emily! How many times…" he yelled.

"I made it," Jackson cut him off. "I'm in a good mood today. Thought I'd be neighbourly."

"I don't take sugar," Mark replied, his voice gruff and not at all neighbourly. "Thanks."

"Thanks, yeah," Jon said. "Sorry. Just shows how often I make the coffee around here. I don't drink it so…"

"I know, I know. Protein power or that limp…" Mark checked himself and changed direction. "Sorry, man. Thanks, really." He tipped the cup in a nod towards his coworker and took another, smaller sip. "Other than the sugar, it's great."

It wasn't, but Jackson was going to have enough to deal with as soon as Tursten Mitchell were in touch. Adding to his rapidly impending misery by moaning about the coffee was pointless.

Jackson held his smile for a few seconds longer, then turned his focus back to the computer screen in front of him. He was wearing black-rimmed glasses, Mark noticed, and wondered if they were a recent addition or whether he just hadn't been paying attention. Five days a week, eight, nine, sometimes ten hours at a time, the two of them sat opposite each other, and Mark still wouldn't have put money on whether Jackson had always worn glasses.

Jackson probably wouldn't have wagered on his colleague setting him up for the pile of crap that he was about to find himself in either, so the men were competing on roughly equal terms.

As Mark Thompson pushed his coffee cup away and tapped out the complex password to log in to his computer, the office door burst open.

It was Thornicroft. Richard Thornicroft, head of InnovaTech. Their manager. Their employer.

The time had come.

Flicking a glance over at Jackson, Mark turned his focus back to his screen. He could feel his pulse quicken and didn't want to give off any sign that he knew what was coming.

"Try to make it look like you're working," he told himself. *"You don't know anything."*

He internally cursed Jackson for ruining the coffee that he could otherwise have used as a prop and considered for a moment picking up the mug anyway. Mark was trying his best to feign an air of nonchalance. Jackson was fixated on their employer, his face flushing, swiftly walking towards their desks.

"Sir?" Jackson straightened himself in his chair in an almost automatic response to his boss's presence.

Richard Thornicroft pulled up beside the two men's desks and stood by the divider like an umpire at a tennis match.

"Don't," he said. "Don't say anything, Jackson."

"Sir?" Jackson said again, the word sounding

more like a question than a greeting on its repeat.

Thompson slowly raised his gaze to watch the exchange of words. Tursten Mitchell must have spoken to Thornicroft. The storm was about to break.

FIVE

Jackson had never been summoned into the CEO's office before. He had expected, of course, that when Tursten Mitchell virtually signed the contract, Thornicroft would want to congratulate him personally on the deal. From the look on his boss's face, though, Jackson doubted he was going to get a pat on the back and a measure of the twenty-year-old whiskey that sat beside the cut crystal glasses in Thornicroft's office.

What had gone wrong? What had he missed? The proposal was perfect. Jackson was certain of that. He had attended to every element of Tursten Mitchell's brief. No corners cut; no expense spared. Jackson had even factored in some of the unpaid overtime that he personally would have to put in to deliver on the account.

The submission was watertight.

So why did Thornicroft look as though their ship had hit an iceberg?

"Jackson," Thornicroft said, as they reached his office. "This was your shot."

Jackson looked at the seat facing Richard, across the desk that now divided them.

"No need to sit," Thornicroft barked. "This won't take long. Don't want you getting too comfortable."

Jackson couldn't conceal his gulp reaction.

Was this it? Was he about to be dismissed?

What had he done? What had he not done?

"Three months, you've had. Three months to get it together and come up with something to impress our biggest client. What could have been our biggest client. Of course, you've blown it. I've been on the phone with Malcolm for two hours already this morning, trying to placate him."

Malcolm was Malcolm Mitchell, and two hours ago was half past seven in the morning. No wonder Thornicroft was pissed. But why? Why had this happened?

Thornicroft twisted his computer screen round so that Jackson could see the email that he had sent the previous evening.

I present for your approval, blah blah

blah.
**Package to be personally delivered,
blah blah blah**.

Jackson scanned every line and then looked
back up at Thornicroft, like a dog staring at his
master, wondering where the ball they just
pretended to throw went to.

"Sir?" he asked, eventually, when Thornicroft
didn't say anything.

Richard Thornicroft leaned forwards, jabbed his
finger at the screen and then at Jackson, prodding
him in the chest so hard that Jackson was sure there
was going to be a circular bruise on his right
pectoral.

He jerked back in stunned amazement.

"Did you get anyone to look at this for you,
before you sent it off?"

Did Mark Thompson hovering over his
shoulder count as a second opinion? He thought
not. Still, perhaps if he mentioned Thompson's
name now, some of the blame for whatever had
happened might be shared.

Jackson shrugged slightly, checked himself,
and stood tall before speaking.

"Thompson checked it over for me," Jackson
said, boldly.

"Thompson," Thornicroft nodded, as though it
was obvious. Of course it was. Mark Thompson
was the only other project manager in the
organisation, and the only other person who

Jackson could have asked.

Had he though? Not really.

"And neither of you noticed you had failed to send the actual bloody documents?"

Jackson visibly deflated, crumbling towards the desk and staring at the screen for the evidence of his omission. There was no friendly little paperclip icon. No attachments added.

"Fu…" Jackson began and caught himself just before he added cursing in front of the head of the company to his misdemeanours.

"I'd say, Jackson." Richard's face was tomato rage red. "Do you know what this contract meant to us?"

Jackson could only nod.

"This would have made us. Our reputation. Our finances. Everything."

Jackson knew. He knew.

"And you and your colleague out there have blown it. You couldn't get it together between the two of you. I should have asked that bloody intern, Shawcross, to work this up. She would have done a better job than the two of you combined."

Jackson almost laughed in derision, but it wasn't the time. Instead, he nodded like a man who had just been told that his dog had to be put down, and himself along with it.

"Why don't you piss off out of my sight? Thompson and you should have a talk and come back to me when you have something to say."

"I'm sor..." Jackson began to apologise.

"That's the last thing I want to hear from you, Jackson. Get the hell out of here. Go."

Thornicroft moved to step around the desk towards him, and Jackson thought for a split second that the two of them were about to come to blows. Thornicroft seemed like a pleasant enough chap, but the kind of balls-up that he and Thompson had made was like a red flag to this bull of a man.

He and Thompson. Of course, Mark could share the blame. Thompson would have no qualms about throwing him under the bus. Why should he correct Thornicroft's assumptions that he and his colleague were partners in this mess?

First, though, before he went back into the office to drop the bad news off at his coworker's door, there was one other person who might help him.

Instead of stepping through into the main office area, Jackson turned into the stairwell and made his way down to level B – the basement, the broom closet, the home of the IT department.

SIX

The IT department at InnovaTech consisted of one thirty-four-year-old man, the only staff member who didn't have to adhere to the otherwise strict suit dress code. Liam Foster's regular wardrobe comprised jeans and a range of T-shirts that ranged from comic book heroes to borderline offensive slogans. That day, he sat with his feet on the desk beside his mouse mat, leaning back on his chair displaying a bright blue long-sleeved shirt that read '*sounds like a you problem*'.

"Hey," Jackson said, trying to sound as upbeat as possible under the circumstances. "I've got a little…" He stopped, looked at Liam's shirt, and picked a different word to end his sentence.

"…issue."

"Well, of course you have," Liam laughed. "Why else would you venture down here into the pits of the building? Not like you've come for a friendly chat, is it?"

Despite his smile, Jackson could hear the snide sarcasm in the techie's voice.

"You know what it's like," Jackson said. "It's one thing after another on the floor. I wish we had more time to…"

Liam raised a hand to stop Jackson mid-sentence, shaking his head.

"Save it," he said, never dropping his grin. "You don't have to give me all the foreplay. Let's just get to the fun part."

Jackson swallowed hard and ran one hand through his dark hair.

"I messed up," he said.

At this, Liam's smile widened, and he swung his legs off the table, sitting forward in his chair.

"And I thought it was going to be another dull day," he said. "So, what have you done, and why is it anything to do with me?"

Jackson let his breath out in one long sigh. Liam appeared to be revelling in his misfortune, and however he described what had happened was only about to compound that.

"The account I was working on. The big one." No point naming names. Liam didn't know one client from another, and almost certainly didn't care. "I was meant to send over the contract and all the pre-account work up and…"

"Stop. Let me guess," Liam interrupted. "It's too easy. Really it is. You wrote a lovely email and forgot to send the attachments, right? That's it, isn't it? From the look on your face, it's got to be." Again, he gave a hollow laugh. "You idiot!"

"Yeah, sure. Hilarious. Can you do anything about it?" There was no way that Jackson could find the internal strength to make light of the situation that was threatening to end his career at InnovaTech.

"So, you wrote the email?"

Jackson nodded.

"And sent it without adding the attachments?"

Again, he nodded.

"And…" Liam paused and made a grand show of thinking about what to say next. "It's too late to send the documents now?"

"Yes," Jackson confirmed, with a hiss of impatience. "The hard deadline was yesterday. They are *pissed*."

"Makes sense," Liam replied. "I would be. And…oh…" He laughed again. "Thornicroft is pissed too, huh?"

"Yes," Jackson said. "I know this is terribly amusing to you, but this is my career. I need…" He didn't know what he needed. He didn't know what he thought the IT guy could do to help him. He was just praying that there was *something* that could be done.

"Obviously I can't time travel, so there's no way we can erase your balls up," Liam smirked. "And you don't need me to send those attachments on to them now. You can send another email, give them what they need and..." He made a hand gesture in the air that didn't mean anything to Jackson.

"And everything would be perfect in a perfect world, sure. But they've already lost faith in me as a project lead and with InnovaTech as a company. They've gone with bloody Si-Nova, and it's too late to do anything about that. I've lost them. I messed up and I've cost this company thousands. Maybe millions. Probably millions."

Jackson cursed under his breath and looked away from the IT expert, unable to face another bout of laughter at his personal expense.

"Oh, mate," Liam said in a tone that didn't sound anything like that of a friend. "That's some oversight, huh?"

Jackson finally raised his voice, stepping towards Liam. "Can you help me or not?"

With a gesture, Liam lifted his arms and pushed his chair backwards, away from Jackson.

"Settle down, suit," he said, finally dropping his smile. When Jackson moved back, Liam gave him a nod, and tapped at the computer. "Change some time stamps, maybe? Make it look like you sent the attachments and, uh, something went wrong?

Some kind of tech issue instead of your mistake?"

Jackson leaned towards the screen, animated. "You can do that?"

The excitement in his voice was palpable and uncontrolled.

Liam pressed the enter key, and the screen was filled with an image of a yellow sign with black writing. It said, '*Zero Days Since Last Incident*'. He hollered with laughter as he looked up at the project manager.

"Best to just get you one of these signs for your office, eh? Idiot!"

Jackson lurched towards his coworker, and the man in the chair kicked off hard against his desk, sending himself rolling across the floor on the chair.

"Dickhead," Jackson barked. "Everything is hilarious, isn't it? How about trying to help?"

Liam rolled towards the door and opened it.

"Time to go, buddy," he said. "Come back next time you can't work out how to switch on your monitor."

"You useless prick," Jackson yelled. "Why don't you just f…"

"Bye now," Liam cut in, waving towards the door.

Jackson stood motionless for a moment, looking the jovial techie dead in the eye before walking past him, out into the stairwell and back up to the office.

SEVEN

Jackson huffed his way back upstairs to the office, seething at the IT guy's shitty attitude.

All he could do was head to his desk, hunker down, and try to think of a way to put right everything that had gone wrong. His years of work at InnovaTech and the reputation he had built through long hours and hard work were crumbling around him.

As he walked into the office, Jackson saw the brassy blonde software engineer, Atkins, perched on the edge of Thompson's desk. She was leaning over, gesticulating in a way that looked neither professional nor businesslike. Her voice was a harsh shriek.

"Sounds like a *you* problem," Jackson mumbled to himself, managing a smile despite his own situation.

Mark was raising his hands defensively, trying to cut in with some kind of explanation, but Karen Atkins kept on firing her verbal shots.

Whatever he had done to piss her off this time had set her on the warpath.

Jackson gave Mark a nod as he took his seat back in front of his monitor. He could duck down, slip in his earphones and focus. All the time he had spent opposite Thompson had trained him to block out the background noise and concentrate on what needed to be done. The only problem now was that he didn't have a clue what he could do to put right his mistake.

If only he'd spotted that he hadn't added the attachment. It was such a rookie error. How could he have sent the document without double, no triple, checking? Thompson. That was how. Pressuring him the whole time; crowding him when he was finalising the email. Thompson had distracted him; everything was that asshole's fault.

Jackson sat, staring into space as the thoughts enveloped him.

The sight of Thompson riled Jackson. For a young man, he didn't make much effort with himself. Always the same suit, navy blue, off the rail. That floppy brown haircut made him look as though he'd kept the same style his mother had chosen for him when he was a kid. There was nothing original or interesting about him.

"Earth to Jacko!" Mark called from across the desk. "You still with us, mate?"

The blonde had left, and Thompson clearly had nothing better to do with his time now than to goad Jackson.

Jackson pretended he hadn't heard, which was his default position when Mark started to make wisecracks. Unlike Thompson, Jackson was serious about his job at InnovaTech. He was a professional - highly qualified with years of experience. Thompson was a smarmy little upstart who…

Something clicked in Jonathan Jackson's brain, and he snapped to attention, glaring over at his colleague.

Mark had been standing behind him when he sent the document.

He was a nosey shit, and there was no way that he wouldn't have noticed that the attachment was missing.

Mark Thompson had to have seen the error that Jackson was about to make.

He had to have seen it, and he had to have kept his mouth shut as Jackson sent the email off to the most important potential client in the company's history.

Mark Thompson had screwed everyone.

And he was going to have to pay.

As Jackson looked at his coworker, he saw the young man's expression change. It switched from the usual sarcastic grin to a perplexed frown to a concerned grimace as Jackson stood and sprinted around the desks.

Within a matter of seconds, the older man was standing beside his colleague, looming over him, mouth open, about to speak.

"Mate..." Mark began.

Jackson shook his head.

"Don't," he said. "Don't say anything. You slimy piece of shit."

Around the office, the project managers' colleagues stopped typing and the usual background murmur of conversation ground to a halt. All eyes turned to the two suits, who appeared to be about to go to war.

"Keep your voice down, man," Mark said, rising to his feet. "Everyone is looking. How about we take this..."

"Outside?" Jackson barked, reaching out towards Mark, as though about to push him back down into his seat.

Thompson jerked backwards and sat in deference. The last thing he needed was to get into a fight with Mr Protein Shake.

"No," Mark said with measured calmness. "A meeting room, maybe. Somewhere private?" He looked around, indicating the spectacle that the two of them were becoming.

"Outside would be more apt, I think," Jackson said with the air of someone who had never been in a physical confrontation with anyone in his life. Still, he leered forward, causing Thompson to push back in his chair, moving away from his irate colleague.

Jackson lifted his arm and stepped forward.

"Mate…" Mark said again.

"You…" Jackson stopped, his hand raised midair, the promised blow hanging. "You knew. You did, didn't you?"

Thompson didn't break eye contact. The adrenaline flooding his system gave him eagle-eye focus. He couldn't let his concentration slip. He had to keep the situation under control.

He said nothing.

"You knew." Jackson's voice became higher, the agitation turning his gravelly tones into a child-like squeal. "You bloody knew."

Mark Thompson's face was fire truck red, his veins pulsating in his temples, despite his attempt to stay calm.

"Did you think I wouldn't work it out?"

Mark licked his lips as though they were painfully dry.

"Do you know what you've done?"

Jackson's voice was almost a scream now.

Mark cleared his throat and said, so quietly that Jackson could barely hear him, "It was your mistake."

He looked the older man in the eye and tilted his head before adding, "...mate."

Jonathan Jackson lurched towards his colleague with full force, aiming a punch at his face. Mark launched his weight against the floor, shooting his chair back into the gangway between the rows of desks, away from the falling blow.

As Jackson righted himself, a booming voice sounded out across the office.

Unmistakably, it was Richard Thornicroft. And he was not happy.

"You." That was Mark. "You." And Jackson.

"You, you, you," Richard pointed at various members of staff as he spoke. "My office now."

Mark stood, holding his hands in a melodramatic pose towards Jackson. Before following Thornicroft's directions, he leant towards his keyboard to lock the computer.

"Leave it," Richard barked. "Now."

"Sir," Thompson said, in submissive deference.

Jackson was rooted to the spot, stricken with a sudden inability to move.

His mouth hung open.

"Jackson! Shut your bloody mouth and go!" Thornicroft snapped.

At his boss's command, Jackson jumped to attention and bowed his head, thinking better of speaking another word, and followed the stream of staff into Thornicroft's office.

EIGHT

The ambiance of Richard Thornicroft's office should have been one of comfort and hospitality. To one side, there was a line of ceiling-to-floor windows, which let in light throughout the working day and gave an impressive view of the city by night. The facing wall was lined with certificates and awards won by InnovaTech and its employees over the years. Thornicroft was rightly proud of all they had achieved. The Tursten Mitchell contract would have been the cherry on the expertly crafted cake. Now, all hope of winning the trust and business of the renowned international organisation was lost.

Thornicroft stood at the head of the long board table and eyed his staff, letting his gaze fall steadily from one to the next. Before him sat the two project managers, Thompson and Jackson, along with five of their colleagues. Atkins, the software engineer, had been summoned to join them, along with Sarah Collins and the intern, whose name none of them could bring to mind. Sitting nonplussed between Jackson and Liam, the IT support, was the research analyst who Jackson had spent so much time with whilst working on the Tursten Mitchell brief, Michael Chen.

"This is ridiculous," Chen said, leaning across to whisper to Jackson. "I don't have time for this. It's nothing to do with me what you suits get up to on the floor."

Liam nodded in agreement with the sentiment. "I keep myself to myself, you know. Whatever you've messed up," he directed the words at Jackson, "it..."

"Sounds like a me problem," Jackson said in a flat, unamused tone. "Yes. I get it."

"It was him?" Sarah piped up from across the table. "What did you do?"

"What didn't he do?" Mark said, with a trace of laughter in his voice.

Thornicroft banged his fist on the desk before him, bringing an instant silence to the room.

"Have you all quite finished?" he boomed. "This," he said, indicating each of them with a wave of his hand around the room, "is exactly why you are here. All of you."

The sheepish intern was a vivid shade of red, her eyes cast down at the table in front of her. The other members of the team looked at each other in curious disgust and distrust.

"I thought you could sort out these petty little squabbles, but obviously I overestimated you," Thornicroft continued. "Thompson. Jackson. The two of you have caused irreparable damage to this company."

Jackson raised his hand and opened his mouth to speak, but Thornicroft cut him off.

"Save it," he said. "Our reputation...my reputation...is on the line. Our company motto is...well, why don't one of you tell me?"

Sarah's eyes flickered, but before she had a chance to speak, the intern gave her response, her eyes not looking up from the woodwork before her.

"Innovation unleashed. Solutions redefined," she said, before glancing an empty-eyed smile at the HR manager.

Sarah responded with an acidic glare.

"Right, yes," Thornicroft said. "And I don't see any innovation or solutions here. All I see is immature infighting and..." He shook his head as he looked again from one person to the next. "...toxicity. That's the bottom line. I have built this company from nothing, and I'm not going to let your pathetic bickering bring it down. I should have stepped in sooner. I saw the warning signs. I've heard the way you speak to each other and the way you speak to me about each other."

Around the room, the coworkers exchanged looks of suspicion.

"Oh, I'm sure that you speak to each other about me, too." Thornicroft let his words sink in for a moment before continuing. "Yes. That's it. You take a good long look at each other. You're all to blame for what has happened. All of you."

Again, Sarah looked as though she wanted to speak, but again, she remained silent. She turned her gaze away from her employer and picked up a pen from the table, desperate for distraction.

"All of you," Thornicroft repeated.

"Sir, I…" Mark stood as he spoke, bringing himself to eye-level with Richard.

Thornicroft moved his hand in a patting motion. "Sit down, Thompson. I can see you quite well enough." When Mark didn't immediately fall back into his chair, Thornicroft locked eyes with him and spoke again. "Down, Thompson."

"Sir," Mark deferred as he returned to his seat.

Jackson made a sharp noise that could almost have been interpreted as a laugh, and quickly reached for a glass of water, covering up his slip with the pretence of a cough.

"This," Thornicroft said, "is exactly what I mean. And it stops now." He bent to the desk before him and handed a bundle of documents to Sarah. "Pass them around," he barked.

Sarah handed the pile to Chen.

"No," Thornicroft said. "Take one for yourself, too."

With a look of surprise, Sarah slid one brochure from the stack and let Michael Chen take hold of the others.

The pile of papers made its way around the table, dwindling as each member of the meeting took their copy.

"Azure Haven Retreat?" Liam said. "What's this? Jackson messes up, and we get sent on holiday?"

"I didn't..." Jackson's protest was cut off.

"A holiday," Thornicroft said with an unimpressed smile. "You could see it like that. I prefer to think of it as an investment. I employed you, each and every one of you. I was the one that interviewed you, brought you into this company, and tried my best to support you. And look what has happened."

The group was silent as they each flicked through the glossy leaflets. On each page were photographs of idyllic pale beaches, clear azure ocean that had doubtless given its name to the resort, and vibrant palm trees.

Intermingled with the tropical images was text that described exactly what Richard Thornicroft had in mind for his employees.

"Have you seen where it is? I can't possibly…"

"You're all going to go. No excuses."

"But my kids. I…" Karen began.

"I've spoken to your, er, *ex*-husband. Everything is arranged."

"Arranged? What do you mean? I can't just…" Karen's indignant tone made her usually refined voice break into a high-pitched squeak.

"You can, and you will."

"But I…" Karen knew it was pointless to continue, so she bit back the rest of her protestation.

"There are two options," Thornicroft said, turning his eyes to look around the room as he spoke. "And this goes for each of you. You commit here and now to making a change, to packing a bag and going to Azure Haven Retreat, or your employment with InnovaTech will be terminated."

"I don't think you can do that," Karen said.

Sarah was already shaking her head. "I'm afraid he can," she said. If anyone knew about the ins and outs of their contracts, it was the human resources know-all.

"You knew he was going to do this?" Karen hissed at the admin worker.

Sarah bit back a smug smile, and instead shrugged. Even though spending a week team building with the office snakes sounded like hell, at least that hell was on a tropical island.

48

Mark rose slightly in his seat, as though he meant to stand, and then settled again before speaking.

"Why would anyone not want to go?" he said. "It's ridiculous that you are even thinking of..."

Richard shook his head, and Mark fell silent.

"Some of your colleagues here have commitments, Thompson. They will leave behind people they love, and you need to respect these differences. We aren't going to have any more of this blinkered mindset." Mark turned his eyes away, as Thornicroft pointed at him. "You will use the time away to get to know each other better, and to learn to understand each other. But most of all, you will develop the team-working skills that every one of you is sorely lacking. There is no room in this organisation for the kind of toxic behaviour that has been festering here. It stops now."

The room was silent. The seven coworkers couldn't bring themselves to face Thornicroft, or each other. Each of them knew that something within the organisation was broken, but none of them had considered that it could have been them.

"Go home," Thornicroft commanded. "Pack what you need for a week away. A car will arrive for you at six am."

The expressions on the teams' faces ranged from indignance to irate resistance to resigned acceptance. Each of them knew, though, that there was no escaping their fate. If they wanted to remain at InnovaTech, they would have to attend Thornicroft's planned retreat.

Hell might be other people, but perhaps in paradise they could work out their differences once and for all.

It wasn't as though there was any other option.

NINE

The team arrived at the airfield the following morning in a dull, uninspired trickle. Jackson was the first to reach the strip, a single cabin bag by his side. Then Atkins and Thompson showed in a shared car, followed by each of the others in turn. By seven am, each of the team was present, apart from Sarah Collins.

"Does she live out of town?" Jackson asked, looking at his watch.

"That a Rolex?" Liam said, craning his neck to see. "Ah, good fake. Nice. Must have still cost a couple of hundred?"

"It's real." Jackson snapped his hand away. "Piss off, will you?"

With a mock gesture of surrender, Liam raised his hands and laughed, turning his head.

No one answered Jackson's question, and the six of them stood on the tarmac, watching the road in for Sarah's arrival.

"I really don't have time for this," Chen sighed, shaking his head.

"That's your catch phrase, isn't it?" Liam joked. "The number of times I've heard you say that."

Chen was stone-faced. "Because it's true," he said. "I actually have an important job to do. Just because I'm not out there on the front line, bringing in clients doesn't mean that what I do is any less critical to our success as a business."

"What is it that a research analyst actually does?" Liam tilted his head.

"I…" Chen spoke, and then shook his head, as though deciding that it was a pointless exercise. "I doubt you would understand," he said instead.

Liam huffed out a short laugh. "Right," he said. "Okay. You probably don't have time to explain anyway."

Chen raised his eyebrows, and for a split-second Liam thought he was going to speak, but Michael turned away, as though suddenly distracted by something far more important.

"We could have had an extra hour in bed," Karen sighed.

"Well, you do need your beauty sleep," Mark needled.

Karen shot an arrow-sharp look in his direction and was about to follow up with a carefully thought-out retort when Sarah's car came into view.

"She's here," Karen said, incredulously. "Well, well."

"That's twenty quid you owe me," Mark said, slapping Jackson on the back. "I knew it."

Jackson grimaced and forced a smile. He reached into his pocket and pulled out his soft calf leather wallet to draw a note.

"Wife happy to see you go?" Mark craned his next to peer at the photograph that popped out as Jackson tugged the twenty free.

Jackson snapped the wallet closed and gave the money to Thompson.

"We've been married for thirty years. I think she can handle me being away for a week."

Mark raised his hands, letting the banknote fly like a flag in the early morning breeze.

"No need to be so defensive," he said. "What happens within your four walls is none of my business."

"You guys want to sit together on the plane?" Liam chipped in. "I can put a word in for you." He followed up with a comedic wink.

"Hilarious," Jackson said, as he slid his wallet back into his pocket. "I don't know why we don't spend more time together, Liam."

Looking on from the sidelines, Karen and Emily

shared a smile before snapping back to their stone-faced solitary positions.

The air hummed with excitement, trepidation, and the heavy aroma of jet fuel.

Before the group, the sleek exterior of the plane shimmered in the early morning sunlight. Thornicroft had patently spared no expense with the luxury jet; he had to be serious about their rehabilitation.

"What now?" Thompson said, looking around.

His question was answered as a tall, well-built man wearing khaki pants and a white short-sleeved shirt descended from the steps of the plane.

The group fell silent and waited for the pilot to speak.

"Good morning, ladies and gentlemen," he said. "My name is Ryan Bellamy, and I will be your pilot today. I've been briefed by your employer, Richard Thornicroft, and told to watch out for any signs of turbulence on the journey."

A murmur of low laughter rippled between the InnovaTech staff.

"It will just be the eight of us on the flight, no stewardess or in-flight entertainment, I'm afraid. The flight should take around three and a half hours. If you need a comfort break, I suggest taking it now."

"There's no bathroom?" Sarah said, not masking the incredulity in her voice.

"You are heading to a luxury, all-expenses paid destination. Each of you has been personally chosen for this opportunity by your employer at great expense. Please take a moment," Bellamy said, looking directly at the HR manager, "to reflect on what a wonderful opportunity this is. Azure Haven is an exclusive resort. This is an exclusive opportunity."

"You certainly like that word," Liam cracked. "I googled this place, and I couldn't find anything about it. What's the deal?"

The pilot didn't respond to Liam's attempt at humour. Instead, he continued with his calm, factual tone.

"Azure Haven Retreat is used by the top organisations, when there is severe disruption or disturbance amongst the workforce. Only a select few are ever invited or welcomed to the island. You certainly can't book it through Expedia."

Finally, the pilot smiled, and a tide of relief washed through the assembled group.

"Now come. Let's get on our way. Those of you with larger cases, I'll stow them at the rear. If you have cabin luggage, take it in with you. Up and away." The pilot gestured towards the steps that led up to the plane.

"Ladies first," the pilot said, standing aside to let the team board.

Karen stepped forward, held onto the handrail, and made her way up into the cabin. As she reached the top, she gave a quick glance below, and noticed Mark looking up at her. Karen shook her head and said nothing, using one hand to hold her skirt to her legs as she steadied herself with the other and stepped onboard.

Emily was next to climb the steps, followed by Sarah.

"Ladies first," Thompson echoed the pilot's words, indicating that Liam go ahead of him.

Liam made a dramatic gesture of rolling his eyes and feigning offence, but he went onto the plane next anyway. There was no point in protesting. Not then.

As each of the remaining team members boarded, Bellamy greeted them at the bottom of the steps with a reassuring smile. Chen, Jackson and finally Mark.

Bellamy stowed the luggage and made his way to the cockpit. The team settled into their seats.

TEN

The pilot's voice was calming and authoritative as he ran through the safety demonstration. For the first time since they had arrived at the airfield, the seven InnovaTech employees were silent, finally listening attentively to Ryan's speech.

Sarah's eyes darted around the plane, familiarising herself with the easiest way to the exit, the best way to reach the emergency life jackets and the location of the oxygen mask release above her chair. She had chosen the front aisle seat, and as soon as she had sat, her seatbelt was in place and fastened.

Thornicroft had them contractually bound to attend any and all personal or interpersonal training that he saw fit, but that didn't mean she had to like it. Travelling to some tropical island was a waste of company resources – the last thing they needed after Jackson had screwed up the Tursten Mitchell deal. They should have been looking to cut costs, maybe even cut Jackson. Sarah cursed herself for not thinking of suggesting this to Richard, and cursed Richard for making her get on an aeroplane.

The murmurs of conversation around her as the plane taxied along the runway conveyed much the same sentiments. No one seemed to be happy with their upcoming luxury retreat. No one apart from Liam, who had arrived wearing a Hawaiian shirt and straw hat and had since donned a pair of red-rimmed shades. He looked ridiculous; unprofessional. Sarah made a note to raise the company dress code with him the moment they landed.

Sarah gripped the soft leather arms to either side of her seat as the pilot ramped up the speed and the plane became airborne.

"Take off and landing are the most dangerous parts of flying," she sighed once the craft had levelled.

Emily, beside her, nodded. "I'd heard that," she agreed.

"Of course, statistically there's a higher chance of one having a fatal accident on the way to the airport than there is being involved in an air crash,"

Sarah continued with a smile that didn't reach her eyes. "So, we are all over the worst of it."

Emily reached a hand onto Sarah's, which was still white knuckling the armrest.

"It's okay," she said in the kind of tone that a mother would use with an anxious toddler. "Nothing's going to happen. You can let go now."

Sarah snatched her hand away from Emily's touch and gave her a piercing glance.

Emily raised her eyebrows and let out a brief sigh before reaching into her bag for a paperback she had brought with her. Sarah didn't want to be seen checking out the title, but could tell it was some kind of business manual. Of course, it was. Emily wanted to give off the impression that she was one of the team; she wasn't. She never would be.

The pilot's voice sounded again. "There's no waitress, but there's a juice for each of you there. Help yourselves whenever you're ready."

"No expense spared," Mark grumbled, picking up the cheap-looking carton and jabbing in the straw.

Above the clouds, the atmosphere shifted. The pilot announced their cruising altitude. The team on board relaxed into their own private bubbles; even Sarah slipped on her headphones and let the sounds of the week's Spotify recommended playlist float through her tense mind.

"I could use the non-existent drinks trolley now," Liam quipped.

"It's not even nine am yet," Jackson chided.

"It's tequila o'clock somewhere," Liam said, wiggling his sunglasses up and down.

"I doubt it's going to be tequila o'clock any time this week, mate," Thompson said, turning around from the row in front. "HR are here to make sure we don't have any fun." He prodded a finger in Sarah's direction, but she was too lost in her music to hear anything he said.

A sudden lurch sent a ripple of tension through the plane.

Karen looked over at Mark.

"Is this normal?" she asked in a hushed whisper.

"Turbulence," he said, patting her gently on the knee. "Happens a lot when you're…"

The end of the sentence was lost as the plane jostled again.

Karen gave a tight-lipped smile, and when Mark removed his hand from her thigh, she smoothed her skirt back down.

"Guys, if your seatbelt isn't fastened, it's time to buckle up," the pilot spoke.

"We aren't all guys," Karen muttered as she reached down to check that her belt was secure.

The pilot either didn't hear her, or chose to ignore the comment, and carried on talking.

"We've just hit a little turbulence. We…"

His sentence was cut off as the plane jolted

60

abruptly. The hum of the engines was replaced by a jagged whirr.

"Nothing to worry about," Mark said, smiling towards Karen, before realising that she was looking away, forward, towards Bellamy.

"Is this...?"

Whatever Karen Atkins was about to ask was lost as the aircraft pitched forward. Gravity pressed against her chest, forcing the words back.

Behind her, Chen couldn't hide his panic-stricken face. There was no way that he could attempt to calm the anxious software engineer when his own heart was beating out of his chest.

The plane trembled violently. A warning siren blared from Bellamy's dash. The floor tilted, and the passengers clung to their armrests.

Outside the small windows, the world spun in a dizzying blur.

The pilot could no longer turn to reassure the colleagues seated behind him. His entire focus was on clenching the controls, trying to level the stricken plane, hopelessly calling for help.

There was no answer.

There was no help.

ELEVEN

The soft caress of sand against Emily's cheek was oddly comforting, like the gentle touch of a loved one's hand. The sun was warm, the sound of the sea soothing, but as Emily's thoughts began to claw their way out of the haze of unconsciousness, the calm gave way to confusion and panic.

Slowly, Emily's eyes fluttered open, and she squinted against the harsh light of the sun. For a moment, all she saw was a blinding expanse of white, and her mind attempted to piece together the fragments of her last memories. The plane. Turbulence. Fear. And then…

The truth came crashing down like a wave.

Blinking rapidly, she tried to make sense of her

surroundings. The turquoise expanse of the ocean stretched before her, its azure waves gently lapping against the shore. Palm trees swayed in a tropical breeze, casting dappled shadows on the sand. It was a paradise, the kind that adorned travel brochures and vacation fantasies.

"No!" she said, quietly.

"No!" she repeated, howling the words as the reality of her situation sank in.

There was no response.

Emily's panicked mind raced, and she looked down, over her body, and out to the sea beyond. Her legs were tucked awkwardly. She tentatively tried to stretch them out. First her left, which was crossed over the other as though she was doing a horizontal Irish dance. It moved. It was stiff, but it moved. Emily allowed herself a sigh of relief before stretching out her right leg. She could still move her limbs. Her back was sore, but her body appeared to be functioning.

"Shit," she muttered beneath her breath. "Shit, shit, shit."

Emily's hands flew to her head, and her fingers came away sticky with blood. There was a dull pounding in her temples, but as she moved her hand back over her scalp, she could find nothing more than a surface graze.

What had happened? How had she ended up there? Had the pilot managed to limp the plane to Azure Haven? Was she the only casualty? Were her colleagues on their way to find her right now?

"Help!" she cried, as the thoughts raced through her aching head. "Over here! Help!"

Emily's heart pounded in her chest, its rhythm a frantic dance of fear and disbelief. She tried to push herself up, but although her arms and legs were seemingly functional, her limbs were heavy and uncooperative. With each movement, her body protested, aching as if every cell bore the weight of the crash.

Finally, she managed to sit upright, the world spinning around her. Emily clutched her head, trying to steady herself as the fragments of her memory collided with the surreal reality before her. The plane had crashed. The team... No one was answering her calls. Where were the others? Were they okay?

Panic clawed at her throat, threatening to suffocate her. She cast frantic glances around, her wide eyes scanning the beach, the ocean, anywhere for a sign of her colleagues. But there was nothing. No trace of the plane, no sound of voices, nothing but the rustling of palm fronds and the crashing of waves.

"No, no, no!" Emily's voice cracked with desperation as she scrambled to her feet. Her legs wobbled beneath her, and she staggered forward, driven by a sheer instinct to find answers, to find anyone. Her steps were unsteady, and she stumbled more than once, the sand seeming to pull her downward as if it wanted to swallow her whole.

Finally, she reached the water's edge, her breath ragged as she scanned the horizon. Tears blurred her vision as her mind grappled with the enormity of the situation. She was – for the time being – alone on a deserted island, her companions missing, her world turned upside down.

A sob tore from Emily's throat, a guttural cry of frustration and despair. She sank back to her knees in the sand, her fingers digging into the coarse grains as if seeking an anchor in this surreal nightmare. And then, as if in response to her anguish, the soft sound of the waves seemed to shift, carrying with it the echoes of distant voices. Emily's head snapped up, her eyes wide as she strained to listen.

They had not forgotten her; they had found her.

Everything was going to be okay.

Or at least it might be, if they could work out what had happened, where they were, and how the hell they were going to get out of there.

TWELVE

Emily raised her hand to shield her eyes from the harsh sunlight as the shadow of a person ran towards her.

"Over here!"

It was a woman's voice, shrill and laced with tense anxiety.

"Hey. Hey! Are you okay?" The woman shouted as she raced towards Emily. Pausing for a moment, she turned around to yell back to unseen figures. "Over here!"

Emily's racing mind hoped for a moment that it was one of the mentors from Azure Haven Retreat, that pilot Bellamy had somehow limped the plane to their destination. But as the figure came into focus, Emily saw the mess of blonde curls that she instantly recognised as belonging to Karen Atkins.

Karen bent and stood with her face close to Emily's, assessing her with a brief visual scan.

"Look at me," Karen demanded. "Look into my eyes."

Emily did as she was told, too shocked and fatigued to argue as Karen continued, asking her to follow a finger with her eyes and then prodding too hard at a graze on her socket.

"Just a scratch," Karen said, as Emily recoiled.

"What's happening?" Emily asked, her voice trembling far more than she had expected. "Where are we?"

"We're in the meeting room, and it's your turn to get the coffee," Karen deadpanned. "Where do you think we are?"

Emily turned her head and scanned the horizon. To one side, the expanse of clear blue water stretched out towards the horizon. To the other, the beach gave way to low dunes, bordered by a line of tropical trees and the beginning of a jungle beyond. As her gaze passed over the sand, she saw a man emerge, followed by a straggle of figures, popping from the tree line.

"Everyone's okay?" Emily asked.

Karen nodded. "Pretty much." She paused, moving back from Emily before asking, "And you're okay? Not hurt? Apart from the..." She pointed at the cut on Emily's face again, causing the intern to jerk back to avoid being touched.

"Woah, easy now," Karen laughed.

Emily felt her face redden, and she instinctively reached up to guard the tiny wound.

"I'm fine," she said. "This is nothing. It's tender, but I don't think there's much wrong with me. Everything seems to work," she smiled, wiggling her toes, and pulling her knees up towards her body. "What about you?"

Karen nodded. "I must have blacked out for a while, but I can't find anything to complain about. You'd think I'd have something to use to get some sympathy out of these guys."

As she finished speaking and gave Emily a smile, the man reached for Karen and put his hand on her shoulder.

"Everything alright?" Mark said. He had taken off his jacket now that they were out in the baking heat and had wrapped his tie around his head like a makeshift sweatband. Emily held back a laugh.

"Fine," Karen said, shrugging him off. "That's all of us then."

Mark turned around and did a perfunctory head count.

Jackson, Chen, the IT guy, Collins, himself, and the two women on the beach beside them. That made seven.

"What about the pilot?" Emily asked. "And the plane? Did we bail out? Did it crash land here? I don't remember anything."

"We hit some turbulence. The plane juddered. I remember the noise; there must have been something wrong with the engine," Mark recounted.

"And then?" Emily said, eyes wide.

"I don't remember," Mark said flatly, turning away.

Karen shook her head. "Me neither. Nobody does."

Emily pushed her hands into the sand and brought herself to her feet. "Maybe if we can find Bellamy, we can get some answers."

Mark shrugged. "No sign of him yet, but that seems like a good plan."

As she stood, Emily took one last look around her. The beach and its surrounds were almost identical to the ones presented in the Azure Haven brochure that Richard Thornicroft had handed to each of them in his office the day before. She had a depressing feeling in the pit of her stomach that she and her colleagues were not about to walk into a tropical island retreat with pina coladas on tap. A team building getaway with the assorted bunch of alpha males, bitchy women, wise cracking Liam and whoever the hell the Chinese doctor was had seemed like a tough slog when she thought they were heading to an organised retreat. Relying on them to survive and save her on a deserted island was a whole different level of awful.

Mark reached his hand out towards Karen, in an

offer to lead her up the beach to where the other members of the team had congregated. Instead of taking it, she walked past without glancing at him. Emily stifled a smile and followed her colleague onwards to begin the search.

THIRTEEN

Jackson was tapping away at his mobile phone when the two women and Mark reached the team.

"I don't think they have 5G in the middle of nowhere yet, Jacko," Mark said, patting him on the shoulder so hard that his phone flew from his hand and landed face down in the sand.

"I said don't call me that," Jackson snarled as he bent to retrieve his mobile. "And for your information," he said as he stood, brushing the grains off the screen, "if we are close enough to the resort, there is every chance that we can pick up a signal from there."

"You think we are on the resort island?" Chen asked, eyebrows raised in incredulity.

"You don't?" Jackson shrugged. "The basic fact here is that none of us knows one way or the other, so we shouldn't assume anything."

"If we had made it to the island, wouldn't the pilot, what's he called, have landed on their airstrip? We would have been stepping out onto the tarmac and being escorted to our own private beach rooms rather than waking up with sand in our..."

Karen shot a fierce look in Mark's direction, and he cut the sentence short.

"You're all assuming that we are on an island. That's how it works in movies. The hapless team are stranded on a deserted island. But we might just be on a peninsula, half an hour's walk from a beach café and an ice-cold beer." Jackson looked from face to face, but each of them bore a blank expression. "All we know for sure is that we are on a beach next to the ocean. We don't know what lies in that direction." He waved a hand inland, past the tree line.

"And we know our plane crashed here," Sarah said.

Chen raised an eyebrow and gave Sarah a long stare. "None of us actually remembers what happened, as far as I'm aware."

"I think we can safely assume that we crash landed here. Bellamy must have worked some kind of magic getting us down," Sarah said. Her tidily tied ponytail had become straggled in the time between the plane and the present. She was usually perfectly presented, but now strands of auburn hair popped out at crazy angles, and her mascara was smudged in black shadow trails beneath her eyes.

"We should definitely look for him," Emily piped up.

"We should find out where we are," Jackson reasserted.

Chen let out a hefty sigh and turned away, looking up the beach.

"Fine," Jackson said. "If none of you want to take me seriously, that's just fine. I propose that a group of us make shelter, and someone comes with me to explore. You're going to look like idiots if we come back with the cocktail menu."

Liam opened his mouth to make a comment and decided against it.

"I'll go," Emily said, raising her hand.

"It could be dangerous," Jackson replied, waving at her to lower her arm. "Chen? Liam?"

"Seems like your colleague Thompson would be the obvious choice," Michael said, nodding in Mark's direction.

Thompson stood thoughtfully for a moment before speaking. "I can go with you. Sure." The last thing he wanted was to have to spend more time in Jackson's company, but perhaps by trekking out with him, they would find help sooner.

Jackson wasn't quick enough to find an excuse to exclude Thompson from the expedition.

"Whatever," he said. "As long as you can keep focus and follow my lead, let's get going."

"As long as you can keep up, old man," Mark said.

"What do *we* do again?" Sarah asked.

"Make shelter. Get a fire going." Jackson was trying to think of the action movies he had watched, but all that kept coming to mind was the television series Lost. "Try not to get abducted by any Others," he laughed to himself as he turned and walked away from the beach.

Mark fiddled with the tie around his head, straightening it so that the long end trailed down his back like a tail.

"Pray for me, compadres," he laughed, as he saluted his coworkers and left them on the beach as he followed Jackson onwards, into the island.

FOURTEEN

Underneath the scorching tropical sun, Jackson and Mark strode away from the shimmering expanse of the pristine beach, their footprints etched in the soft, golden sand behind them. The relentless crash of turquoise waves faded as they ventured further into the lush, untamed heart of the deserted island. Towering palm trees, their fronds dancing lazily in the warm breeze, provided a verdant canopy overhead, casting dappled shadows onto the forest floor. Intricate networks of gnarled mangrove roots intertwined like secret passages, occasionally giving way to reveal the cerulean glint of tidal inlets hidden deeper within the jungle.

With each step, the two men felt the humidity rise, the air thick with the scent of salt, earth, and foliage. The tropical heat bore down on Jonathan Jackson and Mark Thompson as they trudged deeper into the heart of the island. The sweltering moisture clung to their clothes, creating a sense of discomfort that mirrored the palpable tension between them. Since leaving the beach, neither of the men had spoken a word to each other.

Jackson led for a few steps, and then Mark made pace, went ahead. Neither of the two were prepared to accept a follower role. Both wanted to be leader. They strode onward, driven by competitive fire, their footfalls a discordant rhythm amidst the symphony of the island's wild, mysterious beauty.

Amidst the dense tropical foliage, Jackson and Mark moved with an unspoken tension, each step a testament to their unrelenting rivalry. Their eyes, usually fixed on sales reports and quarterly targets, now darted warily between the towering trees, searching for any advantage. When Mark paused to inspect an unusual plant, Jackson seized the opportunity to surge ahead, determined to be the first to find the plane, the pilot, and the prized information.

They were miles away from the polished boardrooms and corporate strategies they were accustomed to, and in this uncharted territory, their competition manifested in the relentless push to outpace one another through the tangled undergrowth. The slap of leaves and the distant cries of undiscovered creatures formed the backdrop to a rivalry that had transformed from a battle for sales supremacy to a potential fight for survival itself.

It wasn't just about survival, though; it was about dominance.

As Jackson moved forward, determined to confirm their location, and prove that they were on the Azure Haven Retreat's isolated beach, Mark followed closely, his eyes scanning the dense jungle for any sign of the crash site. He couldn't bear the thought of Jackson being right. Mark's ego craved the glory of being the hero, the one who uncovered the truth. In doing so, he aimed to outshine his rival once and for all.

After an hour of fruitless thrashing through the jungle, though, they shared a single desire: water.

"Mate," Mark said, from behind. "I need to stop. We should find water."

Jackson walked two further paces before pulling up and turning to look at his colleague. He hadn't wanted to be the first to admit weakness - if the basic human need for hydration could be seen as that.

Instead of speaking a reply, he nodded, sending beads of perspiration spinning towards the forest floor.

"You look rough," Mark said, rubbing his hand over his face. "You need a break, old man?"

Jackson stared at Mark, still not saying a word.

"Mate. We're alone in the middle of a jungle on a bloody deserted island. This isn't one of those monthly catch-up meetings that Thornicroft forces us to go to. This is a bloody disaster. And we are in it together."

Jackson wiped his brow and shook his head.

"How absolutely perfect, eh?" he said. "After the Tursten Mitchell account, I thought everything that could go wrong in my life already had. Looks like I miscalculated."

"Classic Jacko move, isn't it?" Mark goaded.

"Oh, piss off, Thompson. Can't you see that this is why I don't want to talk to you? You're always such a…"

"What? What am I?" Mark had pulled himself up to a straight standing position now. The slouch that walking through the heat had brought on was gone.

Jackson sighed. "I'm not going to start a fight with you, Thompson. It might have been better if someone else had come out here with me, that's all. We're hardly mates, are we, mate?"

Mark felt the fire of confrontation burning in his belly. If there was anywhere that he finally could give Jackson the punch that he deserved, it was then and there. No one was around to see them, and tensions couldn't have run any more razor-sharp.

Mark took a step forward, towards Jackson.

Jackson was about to speak when a loud creaking sound tore through the silence.

Mark stopped dead in his tracks, and Jackson instinctively lifted a finger to his lips. Thompson nodded, and the two of them stood, surveying the surrounding forest without moving or speaking another word.

Jackson's stomach was tied in a knot of unease. He had always been the one to keep a cool head, to stay ahead of Mark, but now, with the stakes higher than ever, he couldn't shake the feeling that something was watching them from the shadows. Something or someone. He couldn't see anything. Still, he managed to conceal his disconcerted thoughts behind a cold façade.

Mark, however, was more transparent. He couldn't hide his fear as the forest closed in around them, the towering trees casting long, ominous shadows. The pressure of their rivalry weighed heavily on him, and he couldn't help but voice his anxiety.

"What was that?" he said in a whispered tone.

Mark's voice wavered, revealing his unease, and he internally cursed himself for displaying weakness.

Shaking his head vehemently, Jackson again put his finger to his lips, emphasising the need for silence. He wanted to pick out any sound that might give him more information about what was happening, but more importantly, if there was something nefarious lurking in the trees, he didn't want it to hear the two of them.

A metallic screech rang out, louder this time, shattering the fragile calm.

"That's not something or someone," Jackson said, his voice a mere breath. "That's the plane."

"What?" Mark's face crumpled into a puzzled frown. "But it sounds…"

"Metal on metal. That noise. I'm sure of it. It must be the plane."

"If it is, it doesn't sound as though it's in a good way," Mark said, still speaking in a hushed whisper.

Jackson's pale, anxious face was undisguisable, but he didn't hesitate. He turned his head in the direction from which the noise had come, and strode off, leaving Mark to scuttle behind him.

FIFTEEN

Left behind on the fringe of the beach and the shadowy jungle, the remaining coworkers stood in mute silence. Their eyes darted nervously between the towering trees and the relentless shoreline behind them. The natural leaders of the team had gone, leaving them to navigate the mysteries of an unknown island alone.

Without Mark and Jackson, the group felt like a ship without a captain, a puzzle missing crucial pieces. While the competition between the two alpha males had often been a source of tension, it had also provided a strange sense of structure and direction at InnovaTech. Now, left to their own devices, the team faced the daunting task of survival without guidance.

Finally, Emily, her trembling hands betraying her anxiety, stepped forward, her voice tinged with a fragile authority. "We need to find shelter," she declared, attempting to rally the disoriented group.

That was the task that they had been given by Jackson, but it seemed that once the men had gone, no one was prepared to make a start on it.

Karen, her usual sarcasm lost in the gravity of their situation, let out a resigned sigh.

"That seems about the strength of it, yes," she agreed.

Liam, the eternal joker, couldn't drop his usual routine.

"So, uh, any suggestions?" he asked, scratching his head in bewilderment. "I've built a mean fort with couch cushions before, but I don't think that's gonna cut it here."

Unabashed, Emily's eyes flitted from one face to another, her own uncertainty masked by determination. She smiled politely at Liam and then faced each of the team.

"We'll need to gather branches and leaves," she began, outlining a plan as anxiety simmered within the group. "A lean-to shelter is our best option for now. It's simple and quick to build."

"How do you know all this?" Sarah said, her words heavy with doubt and distrust.

Emily shrugged and, for a moment, her usual timid expression crept through the bravado that she was trying to display.

"Oh, come on," Chen chimed in. "It's hardly rocket science. We've all watched those documentaries…"

"Speak for yourself," Liam cut in, before Chen shot him down with a sharp glance.

"What Emily says is obvious, but…" he paused, shaking his head. "…she's right."

There was no smugness on the intern's face as Chen backed up her plan. She only nodded, once, emphatically.

"We can't go too far, or the others won't be able to find us when they come back," Sarah said.

"It's probably best to stay on the beach anyway. We can make an SOS sign in the sand in case there's a plane flying over or a boat or something," Karen suggested.

"How many planes have you seen since we've been here?" Chen snapped. "Or boats? I don't think we are in a prime footfall area, Carrie."

"Karen," the blonde said, with acidity in her voice.

"Karen," Chen repeated. "Okay. But still, I haven't seen or heard any signs of life apart from the seven of us."

"Bellamy has to be somewhere, so that will make eight."

"If the suits find him, sure," Liam said. "Jacko had a point, though. We could easily be on a beach at the edge of someone's holiday island or near the

Azure Retreat thing. I know he's a bit of a dumbass, but…"

Sarah laughed, interrupting the IT man.

"Dumbass? What makes you think that? I think he's very smart going off with Thompson, getting away from this bunch of whining…"

"Stop it," Karen snapped. "We are in a shitty situation. We've all been shaken up, even if some of us would like to pretend otherwise. Let's stop the backbiting for a little while and try to do something positive."

"We can start making a fire," Emily repeated her suggestion. "And finding shelter, like Jackson said."

"I suppose fire making is right up your street, too?" Karen challenged, with an unfriendly edge.

This time it was Sarah who commented. "I know you take a lot of unauthorised smoke breaks, love. I'm sure your lighter is going to come in handy for something now."

Karen glared daggers at the HR manager, before fishing in the pocket of her A-line suit skirt and pulling out a silver zippo lighter.

Emily pressed on, ignoring the two women.

"Chen, you and Liam could start gathering…"

"Because we are the only men, you think we should be the ones to do the heavy lifting?"

"Well, yes," Emily said. "And because Doctor Chen seems like he knows what he is doing."

Chen smiled at that, but his grin was snapped

from his face by Liam's next wisecrack.

"What exactly qualifies you as a doctor?" he said, tilting his head as he looked Michael Chen in the eyes. "You're not a medical doctor, so you must be one of those pretend ones with a fancy piece of paper."

Rather than bite back, though, Chen's response was measured. "That's right," he said, stepping forward to pat Liam gently on the head. "I'm one of those made-up doctors that spent seven years studying business analytics to make sure people like you still have a job in places like InnovaTech."

Liam grinned and popped finger guns at Doctor Chen. "Nice one, doc," he laughed.

Chen managed a half smile in return.

"Come on," he said. "Making a shelter will give us something to focus on. We can't be standing around thinking about what a ridiculous mess we are in if we're busy working."

"Oh, I can multitask," Liam half-joked as they made their way away from the group.

"Be careful," Emily called after them.

Chen waved a hand in response and the two men stepped into the trees.

SIXTEEN

As they advanced into the jungle, Jackson strained his ears, trying to identify the direction of the noise. The further the two men walked, the easier it became. The sound of creaking metal grew louder with each step, echoing through the dense vegetation like a ghostly symphony.

Jackson led the way with grim determination. Mark followed closely, his eyes constantly darting to pinpoint any sign of the plane. Although he had submitted to walking behind, he had not yet relinquished the sense of competition that was driving him to catch sight of the target first.

The jungle seemed to close in around the two men. The bottom of their suit trousers was sodden with the moisture of the forest floor; their shirts clung to their chests against the humidity and sweat. Thick vegetation pressed in on them from all sides. The canopy above cast a labyrinth of shadows; the tree roots threatened to topple them with every step.

Still, the men pressed forward.

As they advanced, the screeching became more defined, accompanied by an underlying beat of low rhythmic thumping like the ominous heartbeat of the jungle. Jackson and Thompson didn't speak, but when Jackson turned back to check that his colleague was still behind him, the tension was clear in the glance that they shared. Mark gave a reassuring nod, but still in dire need of water and having too much time with his own thoughts to contemplate the massive pile of shit that they were in, he couldn't manage any further interaction.

Jackson kept his eyes to the ground and his ears finely tuned to the sound.

What would Helena be doing now? What time was it back home? How far away from her was he? Would he ever see her again?

"Stop it," Jackson muttered out loud.

The words were carried away in the thick humidity and never reached Mark.

Thoughts like that should be kept private. Thoughts like that should be kept locked away. Thoughts like that were useless. All there existed in the present moment. They needed water, and they needed to find Bellamy and the plane.

Mark's senses were heightened as he trudged behind Jackson. His mouth was dry, and he longed for a sip of cool water to quench the growing thirst that clawed at his throat.

Suddenly, as they pushed through yet another thicket of vines, Mark's ears caught a different sound—a faint babbling.

"Hey," he half-shouted, half-whispered.

When his colleague turned around, Mark held up a hand, signalling for Jackson to stop.

Thompson's heart raced with newfound hope. Without a word, he veered off the path, following the distant sound.

Jackson, puzzled, followed Mark's lead. As they moved closer to the source of the sound, it grew clearer. It was the unmistakable murmur of a stream, a lifeline of water cutting through the heart of the unforgiving jungle.

Mark reached the edge of the stream, his eyes filled with relief as he knelt to scoop up water with his hands. The mud soaked through his tailored trousers, but Mark didn't give it a second thought. He splashed his face, the cool liquid a balm to his parched skin.

"Jacko," he breathed. "We've got water!" He spoke between gulps, the sweet taste of survival for a few brief moments washing away the acrid tang of fear.

Jackson joined him, cupping the water in his hands and drinking deeply. His weary body and mind had desperately needed hydration.

"Well done, mate," Jackson said, with no trace of irony. For once, he had something to be grateful to Mark for. Their rivalry was insignificant compared to the need for survival.

The two men drank until their thirst was sated; Mark even bent to drink from the stream like a dehydrated dog. Jackson smiled as he watched his colleague, but it was not a time for wisecracks. It was a time to splash the cold, welcome water over his hot, parched skin. Soon they would have to be on their way, but for a short time, the stream offered a brief respite from the harsh realities of the jungle.

The metallic screeching continued: a constant reminder of their mission. Mark and Jackson couldn't afford to rest for long. As they rose to their feet to restart their journey, a different noise echoed through the jungle growth. It was the distant sound of a voice—a voice shouting frantically.

The two men exchanged a glance.

"You heard that?" Jackson said.

He knew what he had heard, but weak from the heat, he had to be sure.

Mark nodded.

"Bellamy?" he said.

Jackson couldn't be certain, of course, but it was the most likely explanation. The words had been lost as the cry echoed through the foliage, but it was, without doubt, a man's voice.

"Let's go," Jackson said.

Mark made a mental note of the location of the stream, fixing in his mind the position of the source of water that could be so important to them and the rest of the team they had left at the beach. Then Thompson tailed his colleague as they advanced in search of the pilot.

SEVENTEEN

Back on the beach, Sarah stood at the edge of the ocean, watching the waves lap against the golden sand. Always one for comfort and practicality, she kept her flat Mary-Janes a few inches away from the incoming salt water. How Karen and Emily were going to cope on the island in their heeled shoes was beyond her. The women who treated the office like a fashion show were going to struggle in their pencil skirts and fitted blouses. Sarah preferred sturdy footwear and Popsy dresses, plain for work, patterned for home.

Behind her, she could hear the two women chatting mindlessly as they assembled driftwood and dry branches into the makings of a fire. Sarah had told them she was going to see if there was anything along the shore that looked as though it might be combustible. Really, she had wanted to be away from the other women; she needed some time alone. Being stranded on a deserted island with six of her colleagues wasn't Sarah Collins's idea of a dream holiday. Having to spend some grown up girl bonding time with Emily and Karen was just about the worst thing she could imagine.

Perhaps not the *worst* thing, but it was close.

Sarah cast a look in the girls' direction. Karen had dragged a hair tie from her seemingly TARDIS-like pocket and was pulling her blonde curls up into a ponytail. Emily, meanwhile, had taken it upon herself to sit down for a break.

They were screwed.

Of all the people to be stuck with, these clueless bimbos were the last on her list.

She turned back to the ocean, scouring the horizon. There had been no sign of ships or aircraft since they had been on the beach. Perhaps they really were in the middle of nowhere. Perhaps they were shit out of luck.

Thirty-eight years old, single, not even a cat to share her home with, and this was how it was going to end.

"Sarah!" Emily's voice rang from up on the dune.

The HR manager kicked a stone into the waves,

watching it tumble into the white-tipped salt water, and reluctantly responded by lifting a hand.

"I've got it started."

Sarah flicked her head around in amazement.

Emily was leaning over the small pile of wood, fanning with her hand.

Leaving the water's edge behind, Sarah clomped purposefully up the beach, trying to get to the makings of a fire before Emily managed to blow it out.

"Not like that," Sarah snapped, as she closed in. "You need to give it some space. It needs time to grow. Back off."

She flapped her hand, batting Emily back from the flame.

Beside them, Karen stood, watching. Clearly never a girl guide, she had nothing to offer other than the lighter that had set fire to the tiny branches and kindling. That was contribution enough.

As Emily sat back, the flame flickered and died. She shot a sharp look at the HR manager, but Sarah was oblivious.

"Shit!" she muttered. "Shit, shit, shit."

"Do we really need a fire?" Karen asked, rather than letting the failure cause her further anxiety.

Emily looked up at her colleague.

"Maybe not now," she said. "But if Mark and Jackson don't somehow come back with a rescue team, we could be looking at spending more than a mini break on this island. The last thing we need is to be trying to find wood and start a fire when it's already dark and we're already cold."

"Shit!" Sarah said again, her voice becoming shrill. "We've put all of our hope into those two trying to find someone to save us. I wouldn't trust them to save a document."

Emily managed a small smile, but their life in the office seemed like a distant memory already. Yesterday's meeting could have taken place in a different lifetime. It was so starkly misaligned with their current predicament.

"We need something more flammable," Karen said. "We don't have firelighters or newspaper. What do we have?"

Sarah shrugged. "My dress has pockets, but they're empty."

Emily's face turned rose-pink.

"I have something," she said. "And it might just be exactly what we need. I'll just have to hope that *I* don't need it later."

Sarah frowned.

"What?" Karen prompted. "Come on, then."

Emily shifted her weight to her left and dug her hand down into her pocket. When she pulled it back, the other two women laughed in unison at what she was holding.

A tampon.

"Well..." Sarah said. "Being female had to come in handy sometime, eh?"

Emily unwrapped the plastic cover and slid the

cotton wool sanitary product out of its applicator.

"Fluff it up," Karen said, crouching beside Emily. "Try to make it as big as you can."

Emily pulled at the cotton wool, expanding the bullet like shape.

"Karen, pour a little of your lighter fluid onto it. Can you do that?" Sarah suggested with sudden excitement.

Karen nodded.

"Put it on those dry twigs," Karen said, showing where she thought was a suitable position.

Emily did as Karen directed.

Karen doused the tampon with lighter fluid, being careful not to waste too much, mindful that they may need to ration what resources they had. Then, when they had laid small pieces of kindling over the top in a tiny wigwam formation, Karen ignited the improvised firelighter.

"Yes!" Sarah squeaked as the tampon burst into flame.

The fire spread quickly to the small pieces of wood, and the women watched as it consumed the larger chunks that would help it establish.

"Well done," Sarah said, in a more motherly tone than she meant.

"Thanks," Emily said, with no trace of admonishment in her voice.

"Thanks," Karen laughed, wanting to share the credit.

"I would say that we all deserve a cup of tea

after that, but I'm all out of Earl Grey," Sarah smiled, sinking to the sand, and sitting with the other women.

Karen's smile dropped. Her voice was suddenly sombre, she replied, "We're also all out of water."

The women looked at each other wordlessly.

EIGHTEEN

Wordlessly, Jackson and Mark followed the sound of the voice, crashing through the underbrush until they reached a small clearing.

There, partially hidden by the thick foliage, lay the wreckage of the plane. Lying pinned beneath the aircraft's wounded wing was Bellamy, covered in dirt and blood, shouting for help.

Jackson picked up his pace and jogged over to the pilot.

"Hey," he said. "Bellamy?"

The pilot nodded, wincing as he moved his head.

"You okay? Let me help you." Jackson reached down to offer the man his hand. "I'm Jon. This is

Mark. The others are back at the beach. All of us made it."

Before Mark could lean to help, Jon gently eased the pilot free.

Bellamy let out an exaggerated, relieved sigh. "That's good to hear." His words came out in pained, breathy gasps. "Very good. And yes," Bellamy said, allowing himself to be helped to his feet. "I'm mostly alright, I think." As he tottered on his feet, he shifted his weight from one leg to the other and shook out his arms. "Nothing broken. Except for this old lady," he continued, gesturing towards the plane.

Jackson turned his attention to the mess of metal.

The left wing that had pinned Bellamy was bent at a jaunty angle; the end of the right was missing. The windshield and front of the cockpit nodded forward towards the ground, ripped from the body of the plane in a jagged tear. One side of the plane had been completely destroyed. The source of the screeching sound was apparent as soon as Jackson saw the fuselage. The cockpit was rocking on the fragile joint that held it, barely, to the rest of the craft.

"That's not our way out of here, then," Jackson said with chagrin.

"The plane is too damaged for me to fly us anywhere, even if this island magically happened to have a runway," Bellamy replied, wincing as though every word was painful to speak.

"It doesn't look particularly damaged," Mark said, tilting his head and running his eyes over the fuselage. The plane was a wreck.

Jackson, not in the mood for jokes, shook his head.

"What happened?" he asked.

"I think we must have had a bird strike." Bellamy shook his head, almost apologetically.

"Bird strike? We hit a bloody bird?" Mark said.

"Well, not exactly," Bellamy said, in the tone of someone explaining something to a five-year-old. "The bird hit us. Or birds, more likely. They can fly into the engine and…" He raised his hands in the motion of a small explosion.

"Let me get this straight," Mark said. "Not one but two birds managed to get into the engine of the - what I assume is wildly expensive - private plane and caused you to crash said plane onto this unknown island."

Bellamy shrugged. "That's about the measure of it," he said.

Mark shook his head. "Doesn't seem right."

"Well, it's not quite," Bellamy said. "I didn't crash the plane. I landed the plane. There's a difference between a crash landing and an emergency landing. I levelled her off and limped her over to the nearest place I could see. And to be frank with you, it's very fortunate that I could see somewhere. Water landings are notoriously, uh, tricky."

"Well, thank you for landing us here," Mark sneered.

"Hey, man. He literally saved our lives. How about giving the guy a break?" Jackson said, stepping up to where his coworker and the pilot were facing off.

Bellamy smiled at Jackson. "Really, it's fine. I don't expect him to understand. We're all in a tense situation here. No one needs to get any more stressed than we already are."

"Uh huh. Thank you very much, oh so wise pilot," Mark snarled, hackles rising.

Jackson threw a stony stare in Mark's direction, making the other man turn his head away.

"Did our luggage make it?" Mark said, changing tack.

"Some of it might have," Bellamy said. "You'll have to look in there." He pointed towards the rear of the plane. "What isn't in the stow might still have made it to the island somewhere."

Mark stepped up to the wreckage.

"Is it safe?" Jackson asked, before moving.

Bellamy nodded. "If she hasn't set on fire so far, I don't think she's going to now. Go ahead. Just watch you don't snag yourself on anything sharp."

Mark reached out to pull himself into the body of the broken plane.

Mark cautiously made his way into the wreckage,

his hands grazing against the jagged metal edges as he manoeuvred through the twisted remains of the once-sleek aircraft. The interior was a chaotic jumble of personal effects, broken seats, and shredded upholstery.

As he rummaged through the debris, Mark found some of their luggage scattered about. Torn bags revealed a mishmash of clothing, toiletries, and travel essentials. It was a stark reminder of the world they had left behind, now reduced to a disarray of material possessions.

Jackson and Bellamy watched him from outside, their faces etched with concern. The plane's structural integrity was compromised, and the creaks and groans it emitted added to the unease that hung in the air like a thick fog.

After what felt like an eternity, Mark emerged from the wreckage, dragging a battered suitcase triumphantly. Over his shoulder was a torn black carryall.

"I found my case," he said, with a wide grin.

Jackson opened his mouth to complain, but stopped before letting any words escape.

Mark dropped the black bag on the ground in front of Bellamy and his colleague.

The pilot smiled, and Jackson looked at him with confusion.

"You know what's in there?" he asked, half-fearing it was a stash of grade A drugs that Bellamy had been tasked with smuggling.

"Of course," Bellamy said. "Show him, Mark."

Thompson unzipped the holdall, and Jackson breathed a sigh of relief as he saw it was packed with bottled water and non-perishable snacks. Nuts, mini pretzels, and corn puffs spilled out onto the clearing floor.

"And I thought there was no drinks trolley," Jackson smirked.

"This isn't going to last you long," Bellamy said. "But I'm sure everyone back at the beach will welcome a snack and a sip of water."

Mark nodded and stuffed the produce back into the bag.

"There were some other cases too," Mark said. "I'll go…"

Before Thompson completed the sentence, there was a whooshing noise from the aircraft, and the wreckage burst into flame.

"Looks like I was wrong," Bellamy winced. "Grab your case. Let's get out of here. This way?"

He hoicked the travel bag onto his shoulder, and the two colleagues looked at each other for a moment before following the pilot back into the jungle, back towards the beach.

NINETEEN

The sun was high in the sky as Chen and Liam returned to the dunes. The women had abandoned the blazing fire for the shade of the tree line, and were sitting, each lost in their own thoughts.

"Good work," Chen said.

Sarah nodded. "Not that we need it yet, but yes," she said. "Thanks."

Emily looked over for a moment and then turned her gaze back out to the ocean.

"Where's the wood? Did you find anything useful?" Sarah asked, rising to her feet.

"Better than that," Liam said, his face animated.

Chen exchanged a glance with Liam before filling in the details.

"We found a cave, not far from here. It seems like a promising spot for shelter. It's relatively dry inside, and there's enough space for all of us to rest comfortably."

Rather than looking pleased, Karen's face fell in concern.

"If there's a dry, comfortable cave nearby, isn't there likely to be something already living in it? Were there any signs of..." She thought for a second. "...life? An animal? There could be bears, tigers, wild dogs, anything."

"It looked pretty empty to me," Liam shrugged. "We have no idea what the local wildlife situation is. Unfortunately, there aren't any signposts around the island to let us know what to expect at the next stop on our safari."

Karen shot a black look at the IT expert.

"There's no need to be like that," Chen said. "We know very little," he continued, addressing Karen. "We should be careful when venturing around the jungle. Staying together would be best. We could implement a buddy system."

"Buddy," Liam said. "I don't really want to implement any systems. You're talking as if we are going to settle on this island and have a long-term plan for our future lives here. I want to get out of here, get home, and go back to my real buddies. Because yes, I have some, and no, they are nothing like you guys."

Liam's outburst was so uncharacteristic that the

others could only stand and look at him.

Eventually, Emily spoke.

"This is a temporary situation, and we need a temporary solution," she said. "If the cave is safe, dry, and even vaguely comfortable, we can use it as a base, and as a shelter. Then we really can start planning, so that we can all get back to our buddies."

She gave Liam a faint, reassuring smile that didn't reach her eyes.

"We don't know if we are going to be on this island for hours, days, weeks..." Karen said.

"Woah!" Liam raised his hands in the air, his anxiety spiralling. "Weeks? You think..."

He stopped, realising as he spoke that none of his colleagues had any kind of answers. They all knew as little as each other. He was no longer an expert; he was just as clueless as the rest of his team. Finally, he had become one of them.

"Let's wait here until Jackson and Thompson get back. They might have found something out there," Sarah suggested.

"I don't know what you're hoping for. You really think Jackson's right and we are a bus ride away from Azure Haven?" Chen snapped.

Sarah shrugged. "I don't know, but wouldn't that be perfect? Why can't we hope for the best?"

"And plan for the worst." Karen completed the adage. "That's what we should do."

A murmur of agreement came from each of the

coworkers.

"We built a fire here, though," Sarah laughed. "What a waste of time."

"It's a signal," Chen said. "A beacon. We can light torches from it, take them through the jungle, use them to start another fire closer to the cave."

Karen nodded. "Maybe one of us should make sure this keeps burning. We need to lookout for any possible means of rescue."

Chen agreed, with a brisk nod. "Yes. When we get to the cave, we can assign roles. As soon as…"

The research analyst's sentence was interrupted by the rustling of leaves and the sound of approaching voices.

Turning towards the noise, the group saw Jonathan Jackson, Mark Thompson and the pilot emerging from the dense foliage. Jackson's expression was sombre, his shirt torn, and dirt was smeared across his face. Thompson too appeared dishevelled, but smiled when he saw his colleagues.

"Look who we found," he said, with a chirpiness to his voice that contradicted Jackson's dark demeanour.

Ryan Bellamy waved a hand in greeting and dropped the holdall on the beach.

"There's not a lot, but here, grab a bottle of water."

Karen scrambled to her feet and sprinted to the bag, tearing the zip open.

"Where…?" she began to ask a question, but stopped, as she pulled the plastic cap off one bottle and drank deeply.

"We found the pilot *and* the plane," Jackson said.

"From the tone of your voice, the water is the best part of that news?" Chen said seriously.

Jackson nodded. "There are a handful of snacks too, but the plane is a no-go. It's wrecked."

"And burning away in an even more impressive fire than you have here," Mark said, nodding at the women's effort, and reaching to take a bottle of water for himself.

"Snacks?" Liam perked up. "You have food?"

"Hmm?" Mark reached into the bag and threw a packet of sour cream mini pretzels in his direction. "Go crazy," he laughed.

The packet was smaller than the palm of Liam's hand. It wasn't going to do any more than take the slightest edge off the man's hunger. Still, it was something.

"Food, water, fire and shelter," Emily said, as though reeling off a shopping list. "We have everything we need for our basic survival."

"For about four hours," Sarah scoffed. "There isn't enough for us to eat or drink beyond that."

"There's a stream," Mark reassured. "We passed it on the way to the plane. It's running water. I'm sure it's drinkable."

"We drank plenty and neither of us have

rampant diarrhoea yet," Jackson said, managing a smile.

"And food? And what about getting the hell out of here?" Sarah's voice became higher pitched as she spoke. "Nothing personal, but I don't particularly want to live out the rest of my days starting a tropical commune with you."

Mark ignored this and turned back to Emily. "Did you say you found shelter?"

Chen filled in the details.

"It's a start," Bellamy finally spoke. "But you really *should* be thinking about how we are going to get off this island. Sarah's right."

Sarah tilted her head with a smug expression.

"Let's get to the cave, make a base and plan what we are going to do next," Bellamy said, seemingly taking the lead.

"That's what I said," Emily agreed.

"We need to take the fire with us," Chen said.

"What?" Mark said, incredulously.

"Torches," he said. "My jacket is over there. You can rip it. Wrap the cloth around a solid piece of wood and carry it with you."

Mark's expression relaxed, and he nodded.

"Good," he said. "Good thinking."

"Get some bark," Emily called over. "Or some moss. Anything dry and combustible. Pack the cloth with it, wrap some of it on the outside too, and see if you can tie it on somehow."

Mark shrugged and pulled his tie from around

his head. Then he stepped over to pick up Chen's discarded and obviously expensive blazer.

"I'll take it," Jackson snapped, reaching out for Chen's suit jacket.

Mark shook his head.

"We need our best, fittest man for this job, grandad," he smiled. "I can do it."

"Grab a log each and stop fighting, ladies." It was Sarah's voice that broke the standoff.

Jackson and Thompson looked each other in the eye.

Mark let go of the jacket and performed a melodramatic bow in front of his colleague.

"You make them. We can both carry them. Fine."

Jackson fashioned two rough torches and lit them from the fire. One he took for himself, the other he stood in the sand for Mark to collect.

"Ready?" Bellamy asked. "To the cave, then?"

"I still think we need to explore further," Jackson said. "We need to work out exactly what we are dealing with here. How stupid are you going to feel if we walk a mile along the coast and find a luxury resort tucked away? We know nothing about this island. Our first task should be to explore."

Bellamy lifted a hand.

"Let's set up a base, and then decide," he said.

Jackson felt the blood flow to his face. He would get no support from Mark or any of his other

112

colleagues. Here on the island, he couldn't run to Thornicroft to voice his dissent. All he could do was comply and wait to have his say.

He was a leader, not a follower, but as Bellamy scooped up the holdall, and beckoned the group onward, there was nothing he could do but go along with them.

TWENTY

The jungle embraced them as they ventured forward, the ominous shadows of the towering trees extending like skeletal fingers over the forest floor. The air was thick with humidity, clinging to their skin like a relentless shroud. The team moved in a tight formation, their senses on high alert, every crackle of a twig underfoot a potential threat.

The journey to the cave had begun, and with each step, the tension built. Every rustle in the undergrowth sent a shiver down their spines. Sarah, Emily, Karen, Chen, Liam, Mark, and Jackson trudged through the tangled foliage alongside Bellamy, the weight of uncertainty heavy on their shoulders.

"Tell me," Chen said, as the pilot walked by his side. "Why do none of us remember landing on the island?" Before Bellamy replied, he added another question. "And why are none of us injured?"

"The second part is simple. I'm a superb pilot." Bellamy gave Chen a sly smile. "I guess the first question comes down to shock, maybe some oxygen deprivation, the work of external forces on your body."

Chen met this with a sceptical stare.

"You have some scratches and bruises between you," Ryan said, turning to indicate the rest of the party. "My guess is that you came out of the plane as I was trying to land. You were probably unconscious before then."

Tilting his head, Chen asked, "So, why weren't you?"

Ryan Bellamy shrugged, seemingly unfazed by Chen's tone. "I'm used to flying, I guess. That must be part of it. Also, I put my oxygen mask on as soon as we started to spin."

"Did you not think it might be a good idea to offer that same courtesy to us?" Sarah interrupted the conversation to have her say.

Bellamy rubbed the back of his neck. The sweat was seeping through his shirt. All of them were suffering from the intense humidity.

"I had to think quickly, very damn quickly, to try to save your lives. Our lives. If I couldn't save myself, there was no way that I could do anything to help the rest of you."

Suddenly Bellamy stopped in his tracks, his body rigid with tension. He raised a hand, motioning for the others to halt.

A low, guttural growl cut through the heavy air.

This wasn't the sound of creaking metal, it was a living creature, and it was close.

Panic surged through the group as their eyes darted first to each other and then in every direction around them, looking for the source of the sound.

"Get close together!" Jackson said.

Simultaneously Mark commanded, "Run!"

The terrified eight froze, none of them knowing which suggestion to follow. Instead of looking at her coworkers, Emily spoke in a hushed tone to the pilot.

"What should we do?" she asked.

Liam grabbed a stick from the forest floor by his side, and, seeing him do this, Chen and Atkins followed suit. Liam looked at the blonde with her dirt-smeared face and ripped blouse with the expression of someone who didn't expect the software engineer to be the one to stand her ground and fight. In return, Karen stared at him with a resolute glare.

"Group together," Jackson said again. "Get in a circle, facing outwards. Girls, pick up a rock."

He pointed at the ground and didn't see Sarah's expression of disgust at being referred to as a *girl*.

Even in the most dangerous of situations, some things could still raise her hackles.

Sarah and Emily both scurried to pick up their makeshift weapons, and the group stood back-to-back waiting, listening for whatever had made the noise.

The growling sounded out again, this time closer. There was an accompanying rustling of the undergrowth, as the threat approached.

"Stand your ground," Jackson said firmly.

Just as he had finished giving his command, a snarling hulking, muscular mass covered in coarse, bristly fur burst from the foliage. Fear and adrenaline surged through the group as the animal charged toward them. It was a dog-sized tusked creature, its eyes ablaze with fury.

"A wild boar," Emily said quietly, her voice trembling.

Rather than run at the phalanx of office workers, the boar appeared to have set its sights on a different target.

With a snarl that revealed its formidable teeth, it locked onto Mark's suitcase, scenting something within that piqued its curiosity. The beast charged forward with a thunderous fury, its powerful frame propelling it toward the suitcase. In a frenzy of gnashing teeth and frenetic energy, it tore into the luggage, rendering the once-pristine bag into a shredded mess, the contents scattered amidst the chaos.

"Shoo!" Mark yelled. "Piss off, will you?"

Jackson snapped round to glare at his colleague. "Shut up!" he said in a loud whisper.

It was too late. The boar lifted his head and stared directly at Thompson.

"Well done," Karen said in a hushed tone. "Dickhead."

Those who had sticks raised them; those with rocks were poised, ready to act. All eyes were upon the boar, waiting for its next move.

TWENTY-ONE

Thompson jerked forwards towards the boar, simultaneously raising the burning torch and pointed stick menacingly.

"Steady!" Bellamy commanded, extending his arms to keep Mark back. "He's not coming for us. Let's not antagonise him."

Thompson shot the pilot a look as sharp as the end of the makeshift weapon he brandished.

"He's just torn through all my gear..."

"At least you had you *gear*," Karen hissed. "What's the deal with that, anyway? What happened to *our* luggage?"

Turning away from the boar for a moment, Mark shook his head. "Now really is *not* the time,

Karen. I'm sorry if you thought your Manolos were going to come to everyone's rescue, but your designer shoes and silly little skirts are gone." He moved his hands in the same gesture of a mock explosion that the pilot had used earlier, and the stick he was holding scraped against his face. "Shit!" he muttered. "Thanks so much, Kaz. Brilliant."

"Oh, for…" Karen began to speak again, but was interrupted by Emily's voice.

"It's turning around," she said, pointing at the boar.

The animal pivoted and made a break for the undergrowth, leaving almost as quickly as it had arrived.

"We're lucky that's the effect you have on males, eh?" Mark said, looking at Karen but rubbing at the scratch he had made on his cheek.

"Dumbass," she said, waving her own stick in his direction.

"Hey," Jackson cut in. "Keep the sticks, but don't be waving them at each other. And quit it with the bitching too, Mark. The last thing we need out here is to be fighting each other."

"Sorry, Dad," Mark said flatly, shaking his head. "Oh, that's right. You're just old enough to *be* my dad, huh?"

Jackson glared at his colleague but didn't rise to the bait.

"Has he really gone?" Emily said, peering into

the jungle to where the boar had run.

"I think so," Bellamy confirmed. "He was probably more scared of us than we were of him."

"I don't know," Mark said, not letting up. "I think I smelt someone here peeing his pants."

"For once, can you just shut the hell up?" Jackson snapped.

"And why don't you tell us the story now about why you have your luggage, and we don't?" Liam said.

"Because he went into the plane," Jackson explained. "He got the water, for which I think we should all be grateful."

"How gracious," Mark smiled.

"And he pulled his own bag out of the wreckage. But..." Jackson said.

"Before I could go back and get your bags, the entire plane set on fire." Mark finished the sentence, with a sad look on his face as though he had really wanted to help everyone but couldn't.

"Of course, you were going to go back in there otherwise," Jackson said in a tone that led everyone to believe that he had no faith in Mark's motives.

"You'd better have saved something good," Liam said, double checking that there was no sign of the beast before walking to crouch beside Mark's destroyed suitcase.

"Hey," Mark protested, thrusting his torch at Karen, and running over to grab the IT man's arm.

"Keep your hands off."

"Fairly sure that what's yours is ours now, Thompson." Liam tugged free of Mark's grip, picked up a T-shirt from the ground and held it up to himself. "You're a little chubbier than I am, but this should be fine."

"You're the only person who is even slightly suitably dressed for the island already," Karen said. "Let one of us have the comfortable, *practical* clothes, eh?"

Liam cast his gaze over the others and threw the T-shirt to Karen. Her blouse was in terrible shape, with a long tear extending down one side.

"If you think I'm putting that on in front of you…" she began, before cutting her sentence short. "I mean thank you. Thanks."

Liam nodded.

"Well, I'm having a T-shirt as well," Mark protested. "They are mine, after all."

Liam shrugged and moved away from the pile of clothes, turning his focus to the other belongings that had been scattered.

"Guys, that boar could come back at any time. Don't you think we should get a move on towards the cave?" Emily pleaded.

Sarah threw a vest in her direction. "Sure," she said. "We probably *should* speed it up a little." Glancing in Liam's direction, she could see Mark trying to move the IT guy away from his things.

"That's enough," Mark said.

"Deodorant, soap...I didn't know you used these," Liam laughed, holding Mark's washbag out of its owner's reach.

"Give it to me."

Mark snatched at the bag, but Liam, although a slimmer man, was taller.

"Condoms?" Liam laughed, waving the strip of three contraceptives for all to see. "Who did you think you were going to get lucky with? It's a work retreat, not an all exclusive singles break, mate."

Jackson joined in with the laughter; Sarah and Karen looked at each other.

Liam threw them back onto the jungle floor. "We won't be needing those, eh?" he said, still laughing.

From behind, Emily's voice rose. "Bring them," she said. "They might be useful."

The coworkers all turned to look at her, but there was no trace of embarrassment on her face.

"Whatever," Liam said, scooping them up and throwing them over to her. "But if you're looking at me, love, I have to tell you now, you're really not my type."

Emily gave the flicker of a polite smile and put the strip of condoms into her pocket.

TWENTY-TWO

Sarah took a small notebook and a pen. Liam salvaged two partially melted Dairy Milk bars. The rest of the group took what spare clothes they could manage, and the rest of Mark's belongings were left behind.

The group moved forward cautiously, the incident with the boar fresh in their minds. The torches were mercifully still burning in Thompson and Jackson's grips. Atkins, Bellamy and the other two men still wielded their sticks, but each of the team scanned the undergrowth and kept their voices low as they walked, for fear that they might miss the warning signs of an ambush.

As they trudged through the dense jungle, Chen

and Liam took to the fore, leading the way to the cave they had discovered. There seemed no doubt in their minds about the direction in which the group should head. With all the disagreement over the contents of Mark's luggage, and who should take possession of what, their shared purpose was a welcome break.

Mark himself was silent, his face stern with the displeasure of having been forced to relinquish his personal belongings to the other members of the team. He chugged on his water bottle and kept his eyes down at the ground, focusing on the path forwards and whatever was spinning around in his mind.

The surrounding jungle seemed more oppressive than ever. Every rustle of leaves and every distant chirp of an unseen animal sent shivers down their spines. Their previous encounter with the boar had shaken their nerves, and those who had them clutched their makeshift weapons with white knuckled determination.

Emily walked in silence, a couple of steps behind Sarah and Karen, who were engaged in a hushed conversation. It was hard to make out their words over the ambient sounds of the jungle, but the tension in their voices was palpable. Emily couldn't help but feel like an outsider, the intern amidst a group of coworkers who were grappling not only with the challenges of survival but also with their own interpersonal dynamics. She stuck her hands into her pockets and felt them rest on the contents with a self-reflective smile.

Jackson and Bellamy had taken position at the back, the men forming an unspoken border at front and rear of the women.

"This is going to sound ridiculous," Jackson said, as they walked, "but has this ever happened to you before?"

Bellamy put his hand over his mouth to contain what might otherwise have been a loud burst of laughter.

"Have I ever been stranded on a deserted island before?" Bellamy asked, eyebrows raised. "It's not something that happens to most people more than once, I wouldn't have thought."

He patted Jackson on the back.

"Have you ever had to crash…I mean, perform an emergency landing before?" Jackson said, unrattled and unsmiling.

"Oh, you're serious?" Bellamy said, changing his expression. "Well, of course, we are trained for such things," he explained. He seemed to think for a moment before continuing. "I had a close call once. I was with an instructor doing advanced training. We were coming in to land and, I don't know, something felt off to me. I told him I needed a go around."

Jackson nodded to show he understood.

"He gave me a firm negative. Told me to land

the bloody plane. I knew, though. We were coming in too steep. Just before we hit the ground, he pulled up on the controls and we made the go around. Stupid bastard could have done for the pair of us. And the company's plane."

"Couldn't you have just followed your instincts?" Jackson asked.

Bellamy shook his head, and beads of sweat flew as it moved.

"I listened to my superior. He made the decision, and I followed it."

"But it was dangerous. He was wrong," Jackson said.

"Yep," Bellamy agreed. "And that was the closest I've come to an accident in my career."

"Until now."

"Until now," Bellamy repeated. "Until now."

After what felt like hours of gruelling trekking, the team finally reached the cave. It was a large, imposing opening in the side of a rocky hill. The entrance was shadowed, and it seemed to swallow the light that dared to enter. As they stepped inside, the interior was cooler than the stifling jungle, and the relief was immediate.

The walls of the cave were damp, and the ground was uneven, but it offered a semblance of safety they hadn't felt since finding themselves on the island.

Although the cave roof was high enough for

even Bellamy, the tallest of the party, to stand, it was only around seven feet wide. They could lie in a line to sleep, but that was going to be their only option.

"Will we all fit in here?" Jackson asked. "To sleep, I mean?"

He stepped towards the rear of the cave, using the torch to illuminate the deeper crevices. It was going to be more of a tight squeeze and less of a comfortable experience than Liam and the doctor had led them to believe.

"Let's get a proper fire going outside again and take stock," Emily said.

Karen nodded, and Sarah smiled in agreement. They had started the fire from scratch on the beach. Lighting a new one from the already blazing torches would be easy. It was a relief amidst a day that had started off badly and had only become worse.

"You could gather some dry leaves and branches for us to sleep on," Emily suggested to Chen and Liam.

"I'll help," Bellamy said, walking to join the two men.

That left Thompson and Jackson without tasks to fulfil. Jackson emerged from the back of the cave looking exhausted and haggard. Mark sat at the entrance to their temporary shelter, looking out into the jungle beyond.

Emily looked over to them, the two people she

had been aspiring to be like, and turned away, leading the other women to a small open area by the cave entrance she knew would be perfect for their firepit.

TWENTY-THREE

Mark's brooding continued long after the fire had been lit. He couldn't shake off the frustration he felt at the group's decision to redistribute his belongings. Each time his gaze landed on Emily, who had inexplicably insisted on keeping his condoms, his scowl deepened. The presence of a young intern, of all people, having possession of his personal items was a dent to his ego he couldn't ignore.

Jackson noticed Mark's sour mood but chose not to engage. He understood that the situation had brought out the worst in some, and he preferred not to fan the flames of tension further. Instead, he glanced at Thompson, who was fidgeting restlessly near the cave entrance.

When Chen and Foster returned with their final pile of covering for the cave floor, Jackson cleared his throat to speak.

"I propose I continue the exploration of the island before the sun falls."

Mark snapped his head up to look at his colleague. In a tone that mocked Jackson's he repeated, "I propose blah blah blah-dy blah. Bloody hell, Jacko, we aren't in a board meeting now. Are you going to get the intern to start taking notes too?"

"Not a bad idea," Jackson said, ignoring Mark's snide remarks and latching onto the useful suggestion he had inadvertently come up with. "Sarah," he said, turning to the HR manager. "You picked up the paper and pen?"

She nodded.

"Can I use them, please? I want to make a map. To be sure that I have covered everywhere, and note down where the stream is, and anything else I might find."

Sarah pointed towards the cave entrance.

"I left them inside. Take them. That's a good idea."

"You shouldn't go alone," Bellamy said.

"I don't think it's a good idea for me to go with him," Jackson said, waving a hand in Mark's direction.

"Exploration isn't really my specialist area,"

Liam said as Bellamy's gaze fell upon him.

Michael Chen spoke slowly, as though deep in thought.

"Your specialist area," he said. "IT, isn't it? You have your mobile phone, Jackson," he said, looking at Jackson. "Can Liam do something with it to help us contact someone?"

The IT expert was already shaking his head before Chen had finished speaking.

"No shakes, I'm afraid," he said. "Short of building a radio transmitter, there's no way we are getting in touch with anyone using a mobile phone."

"You're IT. You must know how to fix things," Jackson said.

Liam leaned back and tilted his head towards the sky.

"I know how to *fix things*," he said, with a sigh that did nothing to hide the condescension in his tone. "If those *things* are your desktop computer, the network back in the office or..."

Jackson cut him off. "You don't need to get smart with me..."

"Liam," Liam said, shaking his head and letting out a sharp laugh. "You don't even know my name. We've been working in the same office for the past eight years. I've *fixed things* for you on a semi-regular basis. You should know my name by now."

"I do. I'm sorry, *Liam*." Jackson pronounced the

man's name with particular emphasis. "I'm not having a very good day, I'm afraid, and I think…"

He stopped midway through the sentence, as he noticed Mark looking over at him with a wide grin.

"Hilarious, Thompson. I'm sure this is all fun and games and boy scouting for you. Here's a news flash: we are stuck here with each other for as long as it takes for us to find someone to get us out of here. And that might be forever. I might never see Helena again. Your colleagues here might never see their loved ones again. And sure, that's fine for you because you have nothing at home to go back to and no one to miss, certainly no one to miss you…but…"

Mark pushed himself to his feet. Already smarting from the loss of his belongings, his expression was of a man tipped over the edge.

"You know what, Jackson? Forget it. You want to be the hero. You want to be the leader. Go ahead." Turning to the rest of the group, he addressed them. "You all want to share my stuff between you and steal everything I own? Go ahead. Screw you all."

"Mark…" Karen said, with shrill anxiety sharpening her voice.

"Mark nothing. Don't think you're special. You never were. You never were, Karen. Screw you. Screw you all."

With that, Mark picked up his torch from where it was resting beside him and strode off into the undergrowth, alone.

"Thompson!" Jackson shouted.

The rest of the team stood and watched, seeming not to know what to say.

"Should someone go after him?" Emily asked to no one in particular.

The pilot answered.

"Maybe he needs to do this by himself," he said.

"More likely he's gone to find a conch," Jackson said, drolly.

But exactly what Mark had to do by himself and where that left the rest of the group was anyone's guess.

Only Karen, her eyes red and moist with budding tears, looked away, and sat back down beside the fire whilst the others watched their colleague thrash his way away from them, into the jungle, into the unknown.

TWENTY-FOUR

As Mark's receding figure disappeared into the dense jungle, an unsettling silence gripped the remaining members of the group. Karen, her face streaked with tears, stared into the flickering fire, her hands trembling as she clutched a stick. Sarah glanced around at the others, her eyes filled with concern.

"What should we do?" she finally asked, breaking the oppressive silence.

Jackson, still holding the pen and paper in his hand, looked at Liam, who shrugged, his expression helpless. Michael Chen's gaze was distant, his thoughts likely consumed by their dire situation. Emily fidgeted nervously, her eyes darting between her colleagues.

It was Bellamy, the pilot, who eventually spoke up. "Let him be for now," he suggested. "Mark needs some time alone to clear his head. We're all under an enormous amount of stress. He'll come back when he's ready."

Emily nodded. "Or as soon as he realises that he's better off sticking with us than being on his own out there."

"I don't think sticking with anyone is one of Mark's strong points," Jackson said, not even trying to hide the animosity in his voice.

"I know you two have had your problems," Emily said. "But if you ever needed a reason to work together, isn't this it?" She indicated the surrounding island.

"Well, it's certainly got you doing more than I've ever seen back at the office," Sarah said. "When I told you that you needed to do something that makes you stand out, I didn't think you'd start acting as the Yoda of the team. You always seem to have the right words now, don't you?"

Emily blinked at Sarah's sudden antagonism.

"I'm trying to keep focused," she said, her voice trembling. "If I stop for a moment to think about what has happened and what might happen to us here, I think I might just…" Emily bit her lip to stop the rest of the sentence coming out. She had been trying her best to appear strong and confident. Revealing her true thoughts would only make her look weak.

"Fall apart, dear?" Sarah said, unkindly. "Well, join the bloody club."

"Look," Karen said. "Fighting isn't going to help. Mark has already gone off. The last thing we need is any more disruption between us. For what it's worth, I agree with Emily. If I start thinking about my kids back home, how they'll be waiting to hear from me…"

"Oh, give it a break, love," Sarah spat. "Do you not think everyone knows about you and Mark? You weren't thinking about your kids when you started screwing him instead of your own husband, were you?"

Liam whispered to Doctor Chen. "Mark and Karen? Did you know?"

Chen tried to bat him away, as though he was another of the mosquitos that were buzzing around in the humid air.

"You miserable old bitch," Karen hissed, rising to a standing position and leaning over Sarah as she talked. "You're just jealous because all you have in your life is your work. You're married to InnovaTech, aren't you? At least the company is screwing you now."

Sarah scrambled to her feet too, and pushed her hands against Karen's chest, sending her reeling. Arms flailing, she fell unceremoniously onto her backside.

"You…" Karen seethed.

Karen leapt back to her feet and ran at the HR manager, her face contorted with rage. Sarah raised her arms, bracing for the impact.

The collision between the two women was a chaotic tangle of limbs and emotions. They grappled with each other, their hands clawing and fingers digging into the fabric of the T-shirts they had only recently salvaged from Mark's luggage. Karen's desperate need to assert herself clashed with Sarah's determination not to yield. The animosity that had simmered beneath the surface of the women's working relationship for so long had finally come to boiling point.

Someone was bound to get hurt.

Sarah managed to pin Karen's shoulders to the ground, her chest heaving with exertion.

"Stop it!" Emily shrieked. "Guys," she said, looking between the men for support. "Do something. Stop them!"

"Maybe they need to fight it out," Liam said with a nonchalant shrug.

Chen's expression was more uncomfortable, but it didn't seem like any assistance was going to come from his direction.

"Jackson," she pleaded.

"Right," he said awkwardly. "Sarah. Karen. Please."

His voice went unheard. Karen was trying to push Sarah off her, panting and sweaty.

"You're wasting your energy," Bellamy said. "Literally."

Sarah turned her head in his direction, and Karen took the opportunity created by Sarah's distraction to give an almighty shove and launch her backwards, away from her.

"Karen," Bellamy said. "You too. You're going to need all the energy you can conserve." His voice was calm and steady, and it seemed to get through to the women.

Karen looked Sarah dead in the eyes.

"When we get home…" she said.

"I'll see you in my office," Sarah replied with a dry smile. "We're on work time."

"You started it," Karen yelled. "There are witnesses." She indicated the other workers, who tried not to make eye contact as she looked between them. "Yeah, thanks a lot, guys."

"Emotional energy counts too," Bellamy said, walking over to Sarah and offering her a hand to lift her to her feet again.

"Thanks," she grunted as she rose.

"It's going to be hard enough for us, without turning on each other," the pilot said, looking first at Karen and then at Sarah as he spoke. "Okay?"

Tears welled in Karen's eyes, partly from pain and partly from the realisation that their discord was endangering them all. She nodded weakly. The others, still stunned by the sudden violence, watched as the tension slowly drained from the two women. Emily felt a profound sense of relief that the confrontation had ended without further harm.

Sarah's anger had not entirely dissipated, but it had transformed into a weariness that mirrored the emotions of the entire group — fear, uncertainty, and the daunting reality of their dire circumstances.

The island was filled with danger, but the demons the team had brought with them were proving to be the most dangerous of all.

TWENTY-FIVE

Mark stormed through the undergrowth, his anger propelling him deeper into the unfamiliar wilderness. He knew he needed to blow off steam, to distance himself from the group that had pushed him to his limits. He muttered curses under his breath, not caring if the jungle heard his frustration.

As he ventured further from the cave, the thick foliage seemed to close in around him. The dense canopy above cast eerie shadows, and every rustle of leaves or snapping twig set his nerves on edge. The jungle like even more of a menacing adversary than Jackson ever had. His steps were uneven, his mind a whirlwind of anger, frustration, and a creeping sense of fear.

"Jackson, you prick," he said as he walked. "This is all your fault. You pathetic bastard. What are you, fifty years old and still need someone to wipe your arse for you? One contract, one enormous contract and you messed it up. Idiot. Bloody idiot."

But Jackson wasn't there to hear him. The heavy undergrowth absorbed his words. He was alone. His initial burst of anger was giving way to something else — uncertainty. He had never been one for the great outdoors. Corporate meetings, spreadsheets, and air-conditioned offices had been his domain. Now, the untamed wild was his reality, and it was closing in on him.

Mark realised he did not know where he was going or what he intended to do. His frustration had driven him away from the group, but it offered no solutions.

Mark's footsteps grew more erratic, and he stumbled over gnarled tree roots and unseen obstacles. His fury ebbed, replaced by a growing sense of unease. The reality of the team's situation settled in — the isolation, the precariousness, the absence of any familiar landmarks. Panic clawed at the edges of his mind.

He paused to catch his breath, his chest heaving. The jungle was eerily silent now, and Mark's bravado began to wane. He realised he had no idea where he was or how to find his way back to the cave. He stopped, leaning against a tree to contemplate his next move.

"What the hell are you doing, mate?" he asked himself.

It was still mid-afternoon. He had eaten the small packet of pretzels and drunk almost all of his water. It wasn't enough. With no long-term plan in mind, at least the short-term goal was clear enough. If he was going to go it alone, he needed to find food and retrace his steps to the stream to refill his bottle.

"And avoid the island's wildlife," he said, out loud, swatting away a mosquito with the palm of his hand.

He tilted his head back against the trunk of the tree, its rough bark digging into his flesh. As he rested, his eyes fell upon the branches overhead. Dangling from a bough, just close enough to reach, was a plump green fruit.

"Mango?" Mark said. "Some kind of tropical apple?"

He tilted his head and to the side, feeling the abrasion of the tree's outer shell against his skin.

A sharp stinging sensation ripped through the back of Mark's scalp.

"Shit!" he said, staggering forward and slapping his hand onto the area that was causing the pain. "Another little vampire sucking bastard bug?" When he brought his hand away, he expected to see the remains of an insect, but there was nothing but a smear of blood and sap.

"You?" He pointed his finger at the tree. "You did that?"

The skin on the back of his head burned, as though he had rubbed salt into an open wound.

"Son of a..." Where the mixture of his and the tree's fluids had contacted the skin on his hand, the red bubble of a blister was forming.

"What the hell?" Mark said, teetering away from the tree.

Thinking quickly, without considering the potential consequences, Mark pulled the lid off his bottle and poured the rest of his precious water over his hand, trying to wash away the sap.

When the water was gone, he looked around, his eyes desperately seeking anything that he could use to wipe off the remainder of the sticky residue.

"Can't get it on my clothes," he muttered to himself, not even trying to conceal the panic in his voice since there was no one to hear him. "Got to find something. Maybe call room service for fresh towels. That's it. Get the doctor on the line." All the time he was talking, he moved around the immediate area, trying to lay his hands on something that might be of use.

The blister on his hand stung more ferociously than the scratch on his head. Both were unbearably painful.

"No fruit for Mark today," he said as he carried

on with the search. "Any tree that stings like a jellyfish can't make any kind of fruit that I want to eat."

He picked out a large dark green leaf that felt cool to the touch and pressed it against the blister. There was almost immediate relief, but still the pain persisted.

"Got to make sure it doesn't get into the cut. Where's Karen when you need a mirror? Always checking her lipstick with that little compact in her purse." He managed to smile to himself as he thought about his colleague, despite his discomfort and heightening fear.

"Karen…" He was wiping the sap away from the back of his head and paused when the thought hit him. "I've got to stop her from eating this. I can't let them…" He scraped the sap away gently. "What if they…?"

His sentences came out half-formed; too many thoughts were flooding his mind. The desire to warn his colleagues about the tree, its burning sap, and the fruit that he was fairly sure could be poisonous conflicted with his anger and the wish to be alone.

"Shit," he said again. "I can't go back. I'm not going back. No, no, no. I'm not going back until I've found a way to get us all off this island. I'll show them…"

What exactly Mark thought he was going to show them was lost as his thoughts trailed off in a different direction.

"Red for danger," he said, his eyes wide. "I'll leave a marker. Smart ass Emily will figure it out, if they even come this way. Crashes on a desert island and finds her balls." He shook his head and set about leaving the warning flag.

The searing pain continued, and Mark was careful not to touch the tree or its discharge again.

"It's not getting worse," he said, as he unbuckled his belt and unzipped his fly. "That's got to be a good sign."

He dropped his trousers and then pulled off his briefs.

"I'm glad you're not here to see this, Jacko," he said, as he stood in the clearing in only his T-shirt, socks, and shoes.

His buttocks were bared to the world, and he lowered a hand to cover his genitals. "Not the damaged hand, Mark," he said to himself. "Getting any of the hell juice on the little prince does *not* seem like a good idea."

While his pants were off, he took a leak toward the tree that had wounded him, not daring to approach it with the bottom half of his body exposed. Then he pulled his suit trousers back on and held his red underpants aloft.

"I claim this clearing in the name of Mark Thompson," he said. Begrudgingly, he added, "And InnovaTech because Thornicroft would no doubt find a way to claim this as his intellectual property. Dickhead."

Then, his face clenched in a reluctant grimace, he stepped just close enough to the mango-apple-demon tree to hang his pants from the lowest of its branches. The care he took to avoid contact with his evil adversary was clinical. He advanced only as far as necessary, and darted back, away from the perimeter of the extended branches, as soon as the scarlet Calvin Kleins were in place.

"Good," he said. "Good work, Thompson."

The feeling of his buttocks and manly body parts against the fabric of his trousers was unfamiliar, but then the entire day had been filled with unusual, unexpected, and uncomfortable experiences.

"How the hell did we end up here?" he asked. "And how the hell are we going to get home?"

Get back to the stream.

Mark looked around.

"Did I think that, or did I say it?"

Stream.

The word echoed through the undergrowth.

"The sap. Must be the sap. Or the dehydration."

There were no signs of any other human, and Mark was relieved to note that there were no signs of any beasts, either.

"At least a tree isn't going to chase after me," he smiled as he walked into the jungle. Then, turning round, just to be sure, he asked, "Is it?"

TWENTY-SIX

Once the tension between Sarah and Karen had dissipated, Jackson took stock of the situation. It was still early afternoon, the sun high in the sky despite their walk across the island and the altercation at their assumed camp.

"I'm going to start mapping the island," he said.

"We really should stick together," Emily cautioned. "Mark should never have left alone. The last thing we need is to lose you, too."

"We haven't lost Mark," Karen said. Her face belied her true feelings.

"No, I didn't mean that," Emily said. "Temporarily. He's just gone temporarily." After Karen's fight with Sarah, the last thing she wanted was to get on the wrong side of the software engineer.

"Someone needs to fetch water. I know where there's a stream. I can map out the island on the way; I'll go farther if I can."

"You'll have to take our water bottles," Chen said with a worried expression. "What will we do while you're away?"

"I...we could..." Jackson struggled to think of a solution.

Emily fished in her pocket and brought out the strip of condoms that she had scavenged from Mark's bag.

"Emily! I hardly think it's the time for..."

Emily laughed at the Chinese man's embarrassment.

"For water," she said. "You can fill one and bring it back. It can hold a lot more than you would think."

"I wouldn't imagine Mark would need extra-large," Jackson muttered.

"They expand, don't they?" Emily smiled. "Take one, maybe two. We might need the other for later."

Jackson raised his eyebrow, wondering what Emily had in mind for the final preservative, and guessing that it wasn't anything to do with intercourse.

"Thanks," he said. "Good idea, Emily. I will take half the water bottles too, okay? Put together what we have left. Who has some?"

The team looked at each other.

"Only a tiny bit," Liam said.

"Not much at all," Chen said, holding out his almost empty bottle.

"Try to conserve what you have. I'll bring more."

"I've got half a bottle," Emily offered.

"Same," Karen said. "I didn't know when there might be more."

The pilot nodded. "Brilliant. Pour the dregs together, and Jackson, you take the empties."

"I still don't think you should go alone," Emily said. "What if that boar is still out there?"

"If there's one boar, there are definitely more than one. At least we know about them now." Jackson was pragmatic about the danger.

"And what about the things we don't know about?" Sarah spoke for the first time since the ruckus with Karen.

"I'll be careful," Jackson said. "I'll be faster alone. I'm fitter than you think, you know."

No one had said otherwise.

"Okay," the pilot said, taking it upon himself to green-light the expedition. "Do you know how to tell which way is north? For the map?"

Jackson shook his head.

"Use your watch," Emily chimed in.

"Someone knows her stuff," Bellamy smiled.

"It's most accurate when the sun is at its highest

point," Emily said. "But we know that was over there." She pointed between the trees to where they had seen the sun earlier that day. "Then find a reference point. The cave will be perfect. I doubt it's going anywhere." She grinned at her own humour and glanced up at the pilot with a sheepish expression, as though looking for reassurance.

"Go on," he said.

"Take your watch. Point the hour hand at the sun. Bisect the difference between the hour hand and twelve."

Jackson did as Emily told him. Around the camp, the rest of the party looked on in interest.

"How does this work?" Sarah marvelled.

Bellamy leaned over to reply. "The sun rises in the east and sets west. Think about your garden at home. South facing?"

Sarah nodded. "I wish I was there."

"If it was midday, you'd have all that lovely sunshine beaming on your lawn. At noon, the sun is due south." Bellamy lay a hand on her shoulder.

"I wonder what direction my garden is from here," she mused, mournfully.

"It's a good job you have one of those analogue watches instead of a smart one. Although I guess they have a compass and GPS built in, so…" Liam laughed.

"My wife bought this for me," Jackson said, his voice reedy. "So, this is our north point," he said, his voice filled with determination.

Emily nodded. "If north is there, you can use that as a reference to draw a map of the island."

"That's amazing," Jackson replied. "I'll use our reference point, the cave, as a starting point. Then, I'll walk back towards the stream, marking any unique landmarks I find and noting their approximate directions relative to the north."

"Fascinating," Chen said, with a look of genuine interest on his face.

"Impressive, Emily," the pilot said, patting her on the shoulder in a way that might have appeared condescending elsewhere, but under the circumstances, brought a wide grin to her face.

Jackson piled the empty bottles into the holdall that Bellamy had brought from the plane and threw the condoms on top.

"Strangest hiking supplies I've ever carried," he smiled.

"Be careful out there, Jackson," Emily said, putting her hand on his.

"Of course," he said. "Careful is my middle name."

Liam turned to Chen and whispered, out of earshot. "If it was, we wouldn't be on this island right now. Thornicroft only sent us because of him."

Unaware of the backbiting, Jackson picked up one stick, threw the carryall onto his shoulder, and started his trek into the dense jungle beyond.

TWENTY-SEVEN

Jonathan Jackson's every step felt heavy as he ventured into the deep folds of the jungle. The surrounding air was thick, a cocktail of sweet and pungent notes. Every inhalation was a dance of sensations—ripe fruits, musty undergrowth, the tang of flowering vines, and the sharp freshness of moss-covered stones. It was almost intoxicating. The air held a thickness that clung to him, heavy with the scents of decaying leaves, blooming flowers, and damp earth. Every breath felt like inhaling a piece of the wild.

The canopy overhead formed a dense tapestry of green. Occasionally, beams of sunlight pierced through, their golden glow illuminating the motley world below. The underbrush was alive with the sound of chirping crickets and buzzing cicadas, their melodies harmonising with the more distant cries of unknown birds.

Jackson was meticulous in his process. Staking the stick into the soft ground and pulling out the notepad and pen they'd recovered from Thompson's bag, he began to sketch. A towering tree with twisted roots resembling ancient serpents, a colossal boulder covered in vibrant moss, any landmark he felt could help the team navigate the island found their way onto his makeshift map. Every so often, he'd stop, scrawling a brief note on the paper.

Each footfall on the jungle's floor, each scribbled note, was a step away from that world of corporate chaos and a step into an unknown one, equally complex in its own right. Here, he was dealing with a different kind of paperwork, but the pen in his hand bore the same word: InnovaTech.

Remembering what Sarah had said during her fight with Karen, he smiled as he looked at the pen.

"We are on work time," he repeated, wryly.

The sun's journey through the sky marked the passage of time, its angle changing the hue and intensity of the light filtering through the canopy. As he delved deeper, so, too, did his thoughts turn inwards. The memory of the missed Tursten Mitchell deal gnawed at him. Mark's intentional omission and the shadows of competition between them played in his mind like a looping film reel.

Mark's subtle betrayal, and the undercurrent of conflict that had defined their relationship seeped into his mind. Their professional rivalry was more than just a battle of sales numbers — it was personal. The jungle, in all its majesty and might, somehow mirrored his inner turmoil. It was beautiful yet menacing, serene, but filled with hidden dangers.

"Thinking about him isn't going to help right now," Jackson told himself.

He needed to be on the lookout for any hazards or threats in the undergrowth. If another boar – or worse – came at him, he needed to be prepared. He gripped the stick more tightly, wondering for a moment whether venturing into the jungle alone had been as foolish as Mark's own solo journey.

It was different, he reasoned. His expedition had the backing of the group. He hadn't stormed off in a childish tantrum; he was on an important mission to create a map, fetch water, maybe he could even bring back food.

Jackson barely dared to voice his greatest hope, but he let the words tumble from his mouth into the hazy air.

"Perhaps I can find rescue."

Although he had rationalised that they needed to be certain that they were alone on the island and hadn't merely crashed on the edge of the Azure Haven Retreat, there was a deeper fear at work in

Jackson's mind. One that he would not reveal to his coworkers.

He didn't want anyone to make a fool of him.

Mark had sensed this chink in his armour not long after Thompson had joined InnovaTech, and he had used Jackson's weakness against him at every opportunity. The pressure of the Tursten Mitchell deal, Jackson's age, even the fact that he and Helena had tried and failed to have children. All of this was fair game for Mark.

The thoughts of Jackson's colleague left a dryness in his mouth that he needed to be rid of.

"I'm going to save us," Jackson said, with renewed confidence. "I'm going to get us out of here."

I'm going to get back to you, Helena.

Back home, she wouldn't even know that anything was wrong. Helena had been so understanding when he told her the night before that he had to leave on a retreat with work. She expected radio silence. She knew how important his job was to him. He missed Helena — her calming presence, her gentle reminders that there was more to life than work. It was her grounded nature that often pulled him back when the rivalry with Mark threatened to consume him.

In the sprawling, unfamiliar jungle, the memories of his life before the crash felt both distant and agonisingly close.

Now wasn't the time to get lost in his emotions.

Shaking off the weight of these memories, Jackson refocused on the task at hand. As he ventured further, the jungle seemed to respond to his presence. At one point, a flurry of brightly coloured birds took flight, their wings shimmering against the diffused sunlight. At another, a curious monkey peered at him from a tree branch, its dark eyes filled with a mix of suspicion and interest.

Despite the underlying anxiety of the situation, there was something inherently calming about the jungle. It represented the wild, the untamed — but also, the pure, the undisturbed. It reminded Jackson that long before boardrooms and corporate rivalries, nature was the original battleground.

"At least I don't have to sit opposite you here," Jackson said with acidic bitterness, the thought of Mark never far from his mind.

As the hours rolled on and the shadows deepened, unease crept back into Jackson's mind. The initial thrill of exploration was gradually replaced with the realisation of how vast and isolating the jungle was. How easy it would be to lose one's way and become just another lost soul amid the green expanse. He looked down at the map, which had stretched over several sheets of paper.

Trees, rocks, clearings.

No evidence in this direction that there was anything other than untouched, indigenous flora and fauna.

No signs of human life.

Jackson was contemplating making his way to the stream for the water refills when suddenly everything changed.

TWENTY-EIGHT

Back at the camp, the cave's dimly lit ambiance was intensified by the sharp contrast between hope and despair. The distant, muted sounds of the island's wildlife blended with the gentle hissing of the fire, punctuated by the sharp snaps of twigs breaking in the flame. The team had made camp here because of its apparent safety from the elements and potential dangers, but there was no safety from the palpable tension that was becoming an even more looming threat than any wild animal.

Liam, trying to infuse a sense of normality into their dire situation, seemed unusually sombre as he began breaking the chocolate bars into equal portions. He counted meticulously, ensuring everyone got a piece, even setting aside rations for Mark and Jackson. Despite the size of the bars, they felt laughably inadequate. Liam looked around, gauging the group's reaction.

"Perhaps we should save this for later?" Karen's voice was tentative, reflecting her concern for the uncertainty of the days ahead.

Sarah's eyes flitted from Karen to the chocolate, her nose wrinkling with distaste. "Of course, you'd say that. Waiting for your lover boy, are we?" The venom in her voice was unmistakable.

Karen's face flashed with anger. "This isn't the time, Sarah. We have bigger problems to deal with. I don't need your petty bitching."

Chen and Liam exchanged a glance.

"The last thing we need is a repeat of your earlier performance, ladies," Chen said with little diplomacy.

"What the doctor is trying to say," Liam cut in, "is that wasting your energy on fighting is…"

"Counterproductive," Chen said, finishing the IT expert's sentence.

"I do know some long words too, you know. Just because I don't have a PhD…" Liam held Michael's chocolate pieces and waved them animatedly.

Sarah laughed and covered her mouth.

"Oh, I'm sorry," she said. "But isn't it ironic that you think Atkins and I should act as though we are best of friends, while you two can bicker away all you like?"

Karen didn't join in with the laughter, but she leaned back against the cave wall in a visible show of relaxation.

Liam smiled and raised his hands in mock surrender. Trying to defuse the tension, he said, "Let's just enjoy this little piece of normalcy, okay? We could all use a moment of respite."

He offered Emily the first piece, a gesture of kindness to the intern who seemed most out of her element.

Emily gave a weak smile, accepting the token. She remembered how, back in the office, the vending machine chocolate had been a sweet reprieve during late work nights. She never imagined rationing a bar on a deserted island.

Ryan, his rugged face illuminated by the fire, watched the team, and gratefully accepted his share of the chocolate.

"It must be super, working on your own," Emily said meekly, trying to bring the pilot into conversation.

"Can't say that today is one of the high points of my career," he smiled.

"Being stuck on this island, or being stuck with us?" Sarah asked, tilting her head.

The question hit each of the team hard. Sarah had meant it as a flippant comment, but the harsh reality stung.

"I barely know any of you," Ryan said, not exactly answering the question. "But maybe you need to find ways to work together." There was an authority in his voice, a hint of something more, but no one could quite place it.

As the group settled into an uneasy silence, they chewed on their meagre rations, each lost in thought. The chocolate, sweet and momentarily uplifting, was a brief respite from the complex web of interpersonal issues that lay beneath the surface. Once a symbol of comfort and indulgence, it now underscored the bitter reality of their predicament. They were a team, yet the divides between them had never been so evident.

In the office or on a deserted island, the InnovaTech employees were the same seven people. The context had shifted dramatically, but their inherent personalities, quirks, and insecurities remained unchanged. The island may have stripped away the comforts and facades of the corporate world, but it only highlighted the underlying dynamics and tensions that had always been there. Now, removed from the bustling environment of deadlines and board meetings, they were forced to confront not only the challenges of survival but also the complex web of their relationships. In this raw, unforgiving landscape, they had the chance to redefine themselves, to rebuild trust, and perhaps, to forge a bond stronger than any team-building retreat could ever hope to achieve.

Or they could tear each other apart.

TWENTY-NINE

Mark felt the oppressive weight of the jungle, the heat sticking to him, sweat pouring down the back of his neck. Every step was laborious, feet sinking into the soft undergrowth, the uneven terrain challenging his every move. The air was heavy, a potent mix of earthy scents, the faint fragrance of flowers, and the slightly metallic tang of his own perspiration.

For the most part, Mark felt alone — intensely, overwhelmingly alone.

He pushed away a curtain of hanging vines, their cool, slightly slimy texture sending shivers down his spine. Despite the stifling heat, a chill danced along the back of his neck. The world felt off-kilter, each shadow too dark, each sound echoing slightly longer than it should. The vibrant greens of the jungle took on a more muted, washed-out hue. He rubbed his eyes, trying to clear his vision.

"Must be dehydration," he murmured, his voice barely audible amidst the soft rustling of leaves. But the pit of his stomach churned with unease, the encounter with the tree playing tricks on his mind.

After the initial burning pain of the tree sap, a cold numbness had settled over the affected areas. He could still feel a throbbing pain, but it was distant, like a heartbeat echoing from afar. This numbed sensation wasn't just limited to his injuries; it was slowly enveloping his entire being.

Mark closed his eyes and focused on his breathing, each exhalation releasing a little more tension. When he opened them again, the world seemed subtly shifted. The verdant foliage appeared in sharper greens, more intense than before. Shadows cast by the afternoon sun seemed to sway and twist, even though there was no breeze. Mark blinked, trying to refocus his vision. Everything was taking on a surreal quality, as if the edges of reality were blurring.

Sweat dripped down the nape of his neck, and he took a moment to swipe it away with the bottom of his grimy T-shirt. The oppressive humidity clung to him like a second skin. Every inhalation felt thick and laborious. There was a weight to the air, a heaviness that wasn't solely because of the tropical climate.

As he ventured deeper into the heart of the jungle, Mark felt a growing unease, as if he were being watched.

At first, it was the faintest of sensations. The hairs on the back of his neck standing up, a shiver travelling down his spine despite the stifling heat. He tried to dismiss it, chalking it up to fatigue and nerves. But then there were sounds—whispers, so soft they might have been the rustling of trees. Laughter, distant and distorted, like a memory echoing from long ago.

The trees are laughing at me. It's following me. It's going to chase me after all.

The thought made no sense.

His feelings made no sense.

"Trees can't move," he said aloud. "Trees can't laugh. Leave me alone. I want to be on my own!"

The distant muffled laughter sounded again, pulling Mark from his reflections. He looked around, trying to discern its origin.

The light filtering through the trees began to play tricks on his eyes. What once appeared to be a simple play of shadow and light now resembled fleeting figures, darting in and out of his peripheral vision. The whispers of the wind began to sound like distant conversations, snatches of words and phrases from his past. Mark shook his head, trying to dispel the encroaching illusions.

"No," he said. Then, with renewed vehemence, he repeated, "No!"

A flicker of movement caught his eye – a little boy running in the distance.

"No," he said again, but this time Mark hardly believed his own refutation.

Mark's footsteps slowed, and he strained his ears, trying to discern if the sounds of laughter, of voices, of his name being called, were real or just figments of his frazzled mind.

Suddenly, the ground beneath him felt firmer, less organic. The familiar crunch of gravel. Mark looked down and found himself on the periphery of a worn-out playground. This place… he knew it. The rusty swing set, the graffiti-covered slide, and there, on a distant bench, a young boy scribbling in a notebook.

Mark recognised the child immediately. There was no mistaking the lonely figure.

He knew him, but it was impossible.

The boy couldn't be sitting there. The playground couldn't be there.

The playground had been demolished when Mark was fifteen years old.

And the boy had grown up to be the man who was standing, dishevelled and dazed, wondering whether he had finally lost his mind.

THIRTY

Back by the cave, the sun filtered through the dense canopy, dappling the ground with patches of light. Emily, Karen, and Sarah sat in a loose triangle around the campfire, each lost in her thoughts. Their faces were intermittently illuminated by the dancing flames. The warmth, however, didn't seem to bridge the chasm of awkwardness between them. They weren't talking, merely existing in a bubble of shared concern.

In the near distance, the muted sounds of Chen and Liam working on the makeshift shelter emanated from the cave's entrance. The two of them had been padding the cave with branches and leaves, transforming it into a semblance of safety.

The air between them was thick with the discomfort of two people who shared a workspace, but not much else. Their current collaboration was born out of necessity rather than camaraderie, and both felt the weight of isolation even as they worked together. They moved mechanically, now and then glancing over at the others. It was clear they felt like outsiders, disconnected from the rest of the group.

Bellamy, perched on a fallen log, broke the silence with a question directed at no one in particular.

"Why do you think Mark has this need to prove himself?" he asked.

Sarah looked up, surprise etched on her face.

"Prove himself? What makes you say that?" Seeming to relish the opportunity to speak, she continued. "Back home, he does nothing but battle with Jackson. The two of them are like a pair of stags locking horns at every opportunity. It's like being a zookeeper, not an HR manager sometimes."

Across the fire, Karen's lips twitched in a rare moment of agreement with Sarah.

"She's right," she chimed in. "He's taken it upon himself to wander off into the jungle. No idea where he is. No clue where he's going. That seems like something an idiot would do, not someone who has something to prove. All he's proving is that he's bloody stupid."

The emotion in her voice was undisguisable, and although Karen tried to maintain an expression of nonchalance, her concern for Mark's safety seeped through.

Bellamy raised an eyebrow, considering Karen's statement.

"Does it?" he asked.

Emily glanced at him, her eyes reflecting the flicker of the flames.

"You think he's gone to find a way to save us?" she said.

The possibility hung in the air like a heavy cloud, making everyone even more aware of Mark's absence.

Sarah snorted. "Save us? Mark? He probably just wanted to get away from all of us, and who can blame him?"

Ryan gave a half-smile. "Maybe. Or maybe he's trying to be the hero. Remember, people act out of character in dire situations."

"With all due respect, Ryan, storming off into the jungle in a strop can hardly be seen as doing something right. Besides, I've worked with Mark for three years and I've never once seen him think of anyone other than himself." Sarah shook her head. "Karen is right. The man is an idiot."

Atkins opened her mouth as though she was about to speak in Mark's defence, but rather than say anything, she let out a long, deep sigh.

Ryan's question had got the women talking, but

Chen and Liam were still on the outskirts of the group, outsiders neither truly a part of nor detached from the team. This conversation, much like the others, felt like it was taking place in a world they didn't quite belong to.

Liam, in an attempt at camaraderie, remarked, "Office politics, huh?"

Chen merely nodded, the weight of their mutual isolation evident in his expression. It seemed he was going to maintain his usual silence, until he looked at Bellamy, and began to speak.

"You must have been somewhat aware of the surroundings when you were landing the plane," Chen said. His tone was like the preamble a barrister might make before aiming a crucial question at a witness. The hush between the other members of the party was electrifying. Chen asked his question. "We definitely aren't on the Azure Haven Island, are we?"

"I'm as certain as I could possibly be that we are not on the island from those glossy brochures. We weren't meant to be there for at least another hour." Ryan didn't move as he replied to the doctor.

"And you just saw a clearing and somehow brought the plane down? Just like that?" Chen's eyes were filled with suspicion. "We crash landed here, and none of us were seriously hurt. Yet none of us remember anything that happened, and none of us were anywhere near the plane when we regained consciousness."

"I appreciate that you're a research scientist, Doctor Chen, but what's with all the questions? What are you suggesting?" the pilot said, with an edge to his voice.

"It's just all very…unusual," Chen replied.

"That's one word for it," Liam laughed, with a nervous edge that wasn't usually present in his mirth. "Listen, we're all alive. I personally am thrilled about that. I've got to get back home so I can keep waiting for them to make season three of 'The OA'."

"Is that all you've got?" Chen snapped.

"A life outside of work where I watch television, play Xbox, and live on delivery fast food and full sugar cola? Is that all I've got? My life? Is that all I've got?"

The silence from the two women, listening with wide eyes, became deeper.

"Liam, I didn't mean…" Chen's face was reddening, and his usual calm tone had been fractured by Liam's outburst.

"This whole thing is messed up, man. I know that. We all know that. What I don't know is whether I'm ever going to be phoning Da Vinci's for a *four seasons* with extra pineapple again. And you know what?"

Chen shook his head.

"I don't care why I wasn't killed in a horrific plane crash. I just want to get home," Liam said, his voice fading back to its smooth, usual timbre.

"I know," Chen said. "Me too."

Karen and Sarah exchanged a look. Despite their acrimony, they shared the same goal.

"Then how about we all try to work together?" Emily said, her voice carrying more authority than it ever had back in the office. "If we could stop making accusations, fighting and backbiting, perhaps we could start to use our energy more productively."

For once, there was no smart remark from Liam. If he had thought of a witty comeback, he had kept it to himself.

At InnovaTech, each of them had focussed upon their own objectives, stopping at nothing to realise them. Their inability to work as a team had been their downfall. If they were going to escape and find a way off the island, things had to change – and each of them knew it.

THIRTY-ONE

Jackson had ventured deep into the dense underbelly of the island. With each step, the makeshift compass around his wrist served as guidance, while his crude map began to take shape. Trees that whispered with the rustle of exotic birds, moss-covered rocks that were slick to touch, clearings that seemed to breathe in the moist, humid air; all were etched into his guide.

There was no sign of civilisation, no hint of Azure Haven Retreat. Only the cacophony of unseen creatures, the distant gurgle of water, and the heady scent of greenery, like nature's very own cologne.

Everything he saw was more of the same. More

trees, more rocks, more overgrown foliage until, as he pushed aside a curtain of hanging vines and stepped into a small clearing, the world seemed to stop.

Partially obscured by wild vegetation was what seemed like an old campsite. His breath caught in his throat as he took in the surreal scene. It was as if the jungle itself had swallowed the remnants of a once-vibrant camp. A skeletal frame fashioned from branches stood at the centre, weathered by time and neglect. Beside it, a fire pit, its embers long extinguished, sat as a lonely testament to the past.

"What the hell?" he muttered, eyes darting around, half-expecting to see a face emerge from the shadows. But the eerie hush, broken only by the distant trickle of water and his own heavy breathing, unnerved him even more.

Jackson's heart raced as he scanned the area for any signs of life, but there were none. If someone had been here, they were long gone. He had been prepared for the possibility of finding signs of human presence on the island, but this camp seemed to defy explanation. The eerie silence that enveloped the clearing sent shivers down his spine.

Carefully, almost reverently, Jackson approached the remnants of the camp. He took a tentative step closer, his curiosity battling his fear. Could there be food amongst the remains of the camp, left there by whoever had found themselves on the island before him and his team?

He moved his hand through the leaves that had gathered beneath the outline of the shelter, motivated by the hunger that was gnarling in his stomach. Never had he so longed for one of his protein shakes.

"But who?" he said, as the reality of his find began to hit home. "Who? And how?"

He sat on a heavy branch that had been placed beside what was once the camp's fire and ran his fingers through his hair.

"Oh, no…" he said as a terrifying thought blossomed in his mind. "If someone found themselves here on a deserted island and they didn't make the news…well…they didn't make it, did they? They never made it home."

The grim realisation dawned on him. Had these campers ever made it out, he surely would've seen their tale on the news or online. His skin felt clammy, his fear palpable. The colour drained from Jackson's face, but there was no one to see it, and even if there was, his pallor was hidden beneath a layer of moist grime.

"They never made it," he repeated.

Jackson threw his head back and looked up at the canopy of branches above. He wanted to scream, but remembering the confrontation with the boar, he managed to keep his primal frustration and fear within.

"Screw this place," he said, instead, rising to his feet and kicking into the pile of leaves, sending them fluttering confetti-like around the clearing.

As the leaves moved, his eye caught a glint of something incongruous on the ground beneath them. At first, his weary, stressed mind could not process what he was seeing, so out of place was it. He bent to shift more of the coverage and confirm what he thought he had found.

"How did you...?"

Jackson spoke to the object that he had found in awed wonder. It was a small, battered notebook, its pages yellowed and dog-eared. The contents were still legible, despite the length of time that the book had likely lain beneath the foliage.

Stumbling back to the log to sit, Jackson leafed through the journal, overwhelmed with his desire to find out more about the island's previous inhabitant – or inhabitants. As his fingers closed around the notebook, Jackson couldn't ignore the profound questions that hung in the humid air. What had happened here? Who had left this camp, and why?

The first few pages were filled with scientific observations, drawings of plants, some of which Jackson recognised. It seemed like this camp once belonged to a researcher or explorer. Then, not even mid-way through the book, the entries abruptly ceased, replaced by haunting emptiness.

"What happened to you?" Jackson asked. "Where did you go? And who the hell were you?"

Jackson's hands shook slightly as he reached the notebook's end. There, scribbled on the inside of the rear cover, was a map.

Jackson pulled his own map out and lay it alongside the one in the back of the book. He could make out some places he had passed on his way to the abandoned camp.

"You are here," he mused, pressing a finger against the mark on the yellowed page that showed his current location.

The island, as drawn by the amateur cartographer, was shaped like an uneven egg. The area Jackson had already covered comprised just over a third of its entirety. Tracing his finger over the pencil-sketched lines, Jackson located the stream that he and Mark had visited earlier in the day, and beyond that there was a neat drawing of a rocky outcrop and an exclamation mark, bold and emphatic.

Jackson turned back to the page before hoping to find a note or a legend that would explain the meaning of the symbol, but there was none. Perhaps if he read through the many pages of information, the answer would be concealed within.

What was most patently clear from the map in the book, though, was the truth that Jackson had been dreading to reveal. The place they had landed was not the Azure Haven Retreat. They were not going to stumble into the luxury resort in the same way that he had stumbled into the derelict camp. If they were going to escape from the island, they were going to have to work out how to do that by themselves.

With renewed purpose, Jackson quickly scribbled down the location of the campsite on his own map.

He sat for a moment in thought, deciding on his next move. The team back at the camp would need water. He had to fill the bottles and return. But, he contemplated, the exclamation mark was close to the stream. A visit to the rocks that the previous inhabitant had drawn wouldn't take him far out of the way. He had been gone less than two hours. If he used the map in the book to find his way back to the cave, perhaps his return journey could be even shorter.

Perhaps there was something there that could be useful. Perhaps from high ground, he could survey the island.

Carefully, Jackson stowed the notebook in the carryall, along with the bottles that were waiting to be filled. Taking one last look around the camp, he stood, shook his head, and made his way onwards.

He had set out from camp with two objectives: map the island and fetch water. The first had been made easier for him, and now the second was going to have to wait. There were more questions than answers, and Jackson had to redress the balance.

THIRTY-TWO

The playground looked just as Mark remembered it: worn-out swings with rusty chains that squeaked eerily in the wind, the old metal slide heated by the sun, and the large sandpit, which had been the stage for countless imaginary adventures. But the most unsettling feature wasn't the equipment — it was the lone boy, engrossed in his notebook, who sat cross-legged on a wooden bench beneath the gnarled oak tree.

As Mark stepped closer, his heart raced with a chilling recognition. The boy's dark, unruly hair, the familiar way he bit his lower lip in concentration, the scribbled doodles on the cover of his notebook — this was no ordinary child. This was most definitely, without question, the nine-year-old Mark Thompson.

The sounds of the playground magnified in Mark's ears. Children's laughter echoed, distorted and distant, but there were no other kids around. The old merry-go-round creaked slowly, turning on its axis even though no one was pushing it. Every detail, every sound was hyper-real, too crisp and defined to be anything but a hallucination.

Mark shook his head.

He scrunched his eyes so tightly shut that when he opened them again, jagged light danced around in front of them.

The scene before him was unchanged.

"How…?" Mark mumbled, quietly. Letting the boy, the younger version of himself, hear his doubt, felt somehow disrespectful. Perhaps that wasn't the correct way to describe it. Rude was the word that came to mind, but that was a word for youth, for playgrounds.

With all the mental strength that he could muster, the thirty-year-old, six-foot-tall version of Mark Thompson stepped onto the playground and walked across to the child.

As Mark stepped closer to the playground, the rusted chains of the swings groaned in a gentle rhythm, as if caressed by an invisible hand. He saw the boy with unruly brown hair, sun-kissed skin, and familiar brown eyes that seemed lost in thought. He wore a worn-out T-shirt that Mark remembered owning, one with a faded image of a rocket ship.

The boy scribbled fervently into his small notebook. Mark remembered that notebook. It was where he penned down his dreams, fears, and secrets. Those writings were the purest reflection of his soul back then.

"Hey," Mark said hesitantly, when he reached the boy, his voice cracking with anxiety. "What are you writing?"

The boy didn't look up. The only sign he heard was a slight stiffening of his posture. But then, without raising his head, he responded, "Things that mustn't be forgotten."

Every word echoed in Mark's ears, a resonance that seemed both alien and deeply personal. The weight of the boy's statement pushed down on him, and the surrounding playground grew more vivid, more tactile.

Mark looked towards the merry-go-round, the one he and his friends had spent countless hours on, pushing each other faster and faster until the world blurred. But now, it stood still, its paint chipped, revealing the silver bones beneath. There was an eerie stillness to it, a stark contrast to the lively memories Mark held of it.

The slide, once shiny and red, now had a veneer of rust. The sandbox, where he'd built castles and dug moats, seemed untouched by time, but a quick glance told him the toys he once played with were nowhere to be seen.

Suddenly, a distant laughter echoed, pulling Mark's attention. Shadowy figures of children ran past him, their features blurred, their laughter both joyous and haunting. Among them, he spotted a younger version of his childhood friend, Lucy, her golden locks flowing behind her as she chased after another silhouette.

"Lucy?"

But she couldn't be here. She had moved away when they were teenagers, their paths diverging like the branches of the giant oaks surrounding the playground. Yet, here she was, a ghost from his past.

A chilling wind blew, and Mark felt a hand tug at his arm. Turning, he stared into the eyes of his younger self, those innocent brown eyes now clouded with a mix of fear and urgency.

"You have to remember," the boy whispered, his grip tightening. "You have to end it."

"End what?" Mark asked, panic clear in his voice.

The weight of forgotten memories and buried guilt pressed down on Mark. He remembered the notebook. It was where he had written his dreams, aspirations, and fears. He recalled nights spent under the stars, scribbling away, dreaming of a future full of promise.

But what had he forgotten? What did he have to end?

The surrounding scene began to shift. The once bright sky turned overcast. The rusted playground equipment decayed further, morphing into grotesque shapes, their outlines shimmering and distorting. Shadows lengthened and retreated, and the whispers grew louder, more urgent.

Images flashed before Mark's eyes: birthdays, first days of school, family gatherings. But amid these memories, there were darker moments. Arguments with parents, betrayals by friends, moments of intense fear, and a paralysing sense of loneliness.

He saw himself as a teenager, standing at the edge of the playground, looking at the construction vehicles ready to tear it down.

Suddenly, the boy was in front of him, gripping Mark's arms with a desperate intensity. "End it!" he shouted, just as the world around Mark dissolved, the colours bleeding into one another.

THIRTY-THREE

The group around the campsite had reverted to a still silence, but the tension in the air had lessened. Michael and Liam pressed on with their task of bringing comfort to the cave without sharing a word. Emily and Karen occupied a log close to the fire, whilst Sarah kept her distance from them, whether planned or unplanned, sitting on a low, flat rock.

With no written agenda, no key performance indicators to meet and no InnovaTech business to carry out, it seemed the group had little to say to each other. The jungle around them and the need to escape the dire situation they were in seemed to be all they had in common, and for the moment, no one wanted to talk about it.

Finally breaking the silence, Sarah abruptly stood.

"I need to use the restroom," she said. "Or, well, find a secluded spot."

She gestured vaguely towards the dense undergrowth on the outskirts of their camp.

Karen, showing an unexpected side of concern, looked at the HR manager and said, "It's not safe out there alone. One of us should go with you." She stopped short of volunteering her own company.

Sarah rolled her eyes, her usual assertive demeanour shining through. "I think I'm old enough to handle a trip to the toilet. Thank you."

Overhearing the conversation, Liam, pausing from his task, pointed out a simple fact.

"You can't very well fend off a wild boar when you're... occupied."

"Oh, for heaven's sake," Sarah huffed, ready to argue, but Emily interjected, standing and brushing dirt off her pants.

"I'll go with you, Sarah," she said. "Better safe than sorry."

The HR manager hesitated, searching Emily's face, then gave a reluctant nod.

"Fine. But if you tell anyone about my jungle bathroom habits, I'll have you written up for privacy violations," she joked weakly, attempting to lighten the mood.

Emily jumped at the opportunity to gain favour with Sarah.

"We're all on the clock here, I know," she said with a smile.

"Just...be careful," Chen said, his voice trembling slightly.

"Don't go out of earshot. If anything happens, shout and we'll be with you in no time. And Emily, take one of the sticks," Liam said in an uncharacteristically sensible moment.

Nodding, Emily picked up the nearest weapon. Fighting boar hadn't been listed in her appointments calendar for the day, and she hoped that no wild animals could find an open slot in their agenda to give either of them any trouble.

"Strength in numbers," Emily said, trying to maintain her smile.

"Anything at all," Liam reiterated sternly.

Sarah shook her head.

"This is a little ridiculous," she said, irritation clear in her voice.

She strode away from the camp, out into the bush, and Emily picked up her pace to follow.

The two women ventured into the dense foliage. As they walked side by side, the chirping of cicadas grew louder, and the scent of damp earth filled the air. The canopy of trees engulfed Sarah and Emily in a cocoon of subdued light and stifling silence. Every step further into the jungle seemed to separate them more from the world they knew and intensify the gulf that had recently formed between them.

"You'd think," Sarah began, her voice cool and detached, "with all your clever little survival skills and oh-so-clever ideas, you'd have a way of making yourself stand out at the office."

Emily's thoughts swirled back to that humiliating meeting with Sarah. The cold dismissal of her inquiry, Sarah's demeaning undertone—every word was etched in her memory.

Emily's face tightened, but she took a steadying breath before replying. "I came to you in good faith, Sarah. Looking for guidance. Not everyone gets handed their position on a silver platter."

Sarah raised an eyebrow, amusement clear in her gaze. "Oh, trust me, I've earned every bit of where I am. Maybe if you spent less time daydreaming and more time working, you wouldn't need to trail behind Jackson and Thompson."

"I just thought that you would—" Emily started, but Sarah cut her off.

"That I would what? Hand you a job because you asked nicely?"

Emily bit her lip, holding back a retort. The weight of their isolation, the inherent danger around them, seemed to amplify their differences rather than bridge them.

"I just wanted a fair chance," Emily whispered, more to herself than to Sarah.

Sarah's pace slowed, and she took a deep breath. "Look, Emily, survival here is the priority. And sometimes, survival in a corporate jungle isn't much different. You have to stand out, make your mark. Right now, we need to focus. Personal grievances have to wait."

Emily swallowed her retort. "Fine," she murmured, feeling the sting of their recent encounter all over again.

Suddenly, Sarah paused, taking a moment to survey the terrain.

"This should do," she said, pointing to a slightly cleared area surrounded by dense foliage. "Stay here. I won't be long."

Emily nodded, the undercurrents of their conversation still lingering as she watched Sarah disappear into the vegetation.

The young intern idly played with a fallen leaf, tearing it into neat little pieces while she waited. The sounds of the jungle, both near and distant, formed a consistent backdrop of chirping, rustling, and the occasional distant animal call.

As she stood, Emily's anxiety and resentment intermingled, creating a cocktail of conflicting emotions. The jungle's omnipresent sounds seemed to grow louder in Sarah's absence. She tried to focus on the patterns the sunlight made as it filtered through the trees, but her thoughts kept wandering back to Sarah's prolonged absence.

"Probably lecturing some plant about its professional growth," she mused with a forced chuckle.

Time seemed to stretch. Emily's patience turned into discomfort, and then into worry.

"Sarah?" she called. "Are you okay?"

Half-expecting Sarah to shout back, telling her to shut up and stop interrupting her flow, Emily's words came out more timidly than she had planned.

"Sarah?" she shouted again when there was no reply.

Silence.

"Sarah, come on! This isn't funny!"

Emily's voice trembled, betraying her growing fear. She hoped it was a cruel joke, or perhaps Sarah had simply wandered farther to find a more private spot.

Straining her ears for any sign, Emily slowly approached the spot where Sarah had walked into the undergrowth. She scanned the ground, trying to discern Sarah's footprints from the countless other imprints. But the jungle floor revealed nothing.

Panic gripped Emily as every horror story she'd ever heard about missing people in the wild raced through her mind.

"SARAH!" she screamed, her voice breaking.

"SARAH, ANSWER ME!"

Her heart thundered as the awful possibilities cascaded through her mind. Had Sarah had an accident? Was there something — or someone — in the jungle with them? The isolation, the uncertainty, the darkness closing in around her; it all became too much. The oppressive air felt suffocating, the dense canopy above blocking any comfort the sky might have provided. Emily felt small and utterly alone.

With terror taking hold, Emily turned on her heel and ran towards the camp, branches scratching her face and arms. Her screams cut through the stillness as she cried out, desperate for help from the rest of the team.

"Help! Someone! Please! SARAH'S GONE!"

THIRTY-FOUR

Jackson left the remnants of the abandoned camp behind, the weight of the journal in his carryall a tangible reminder of the island's secrets. The birds sang a discordant melody overhead, a cacophony that was both alien and mesmerising. Their shrill calls were the only sign of life as he ventured deeper into the dense forest.

Now and then, he would stop, take a deep breath, and press onward. He was getting older, no matter how he tried to ignore it, it was inescapable. The dry heat pressed down on him; the relentless afternoon sun sought to sap his strength. His body, though not yet parched with thirst, quietly urged him toward the stream, a primal instinct to seek sustenance. The rest of the group, back at the cave, might already be feeling the desperate pangs of dehydration. He had to make a choice.

On one hand, he could visit the stream first, fill the bottles and the makeshift water bags and take them back to the team. They could survive on what they had for a while, but for how long? On the other hand, the rocks shown on the map he had found in the journal could allow him to reach high ground, survey the island from a vantage point, and find a means of escape.

If he took the water to the camp, there would be no time to return and venture to the rocky heights before sunset. Being stranded on a deserted island was bad enough without being lost on a cliff in the dark. He had to think. He had to manage the risks. That was his job, after all; planning and strategic thinking were his livelihood. Now those skills could save his life.

He had to get home. He had to get back to Helena.

The thought of water fresh in his mind, Jackson paused for a brief break from the relentless walk and to drink what was left in his bottle. There was so little that it barely dampened his mouth. Stopping at the stream was a must, even if he chose to press on further before returning to camp. Before pressing on, Jackson reached into his pocket and pulled out the leather wallet that had been a gift from his wife. It seemed that so many of the things that he loved and prized had been gifts from his wife. She knew him so well and loved him so deeply. What had he ever given her in return?

Jackson slid the image of a younger Mr and Mrs Jackson out from its leather home and held it in the palm of his hand. The day the photograph had been taken, the couple had been on a trip around Italy. Helena wanted to visit the Uffizi, desperate to see The Birth of Venus, but Jackson had insisted they stop for gelato in the square. It was a hot day in Florence, but nothing compared to the heat of the jungle that Jackson had spent the day battling against. Helena had caved to Jackson's incessant wheedling, and she had bought them both cones overfull with creamy pistachio. Helena's Italian was poor, but better than her husband's. She always handled communication with the locals. Jackson still remembered the sweet smooth taste of the gelato that they ate as they made their way across the Piazza della Signoria.

Finally reaching the doors of the gallery, they realised that Helena's purse had been lifted from her bag. It must have happened somewhere between the gelateria and the gallery. If Jackson hadn't been so insistent on getting what he wanted, it would never have happened. Helena spent the afternoon trying to explain to the police what had happened, using her broken BBC phrase-book Italian. They never made it to the gallery. She never saw the Botticelli. Jackson had never eaten ice cream since.

Yet this was the photograph that Jackson chose to keep in his wallet.

Jackson ran his finger over the image of his wife.

The man that he was now worked hard for Helena. The man he was now gave her everything she could dream of.

And Mark Thompson stood to bring all of that to a crashing halt.

Mark Thompson, the stupid, selfish prick, was more concerned about getting one up on him in the office than working as a team to succeed.

Mark Thompson was a childish, pathetic loser who had stormed off into the jungle because he couldn't share what he had to help his workmates.

Mark Thompson was the reason that he was here, now, on the island, miles away from home. Miles away from Helena.

The photograph in Jackson's hand was a tangible connection to the life to which he so desperately wanted to return.

He wouldn't let Mark Thompson dictate the outcome of his story. Jackson made up his mind. He would visit the stream first, fill his water bottles, and then ascend those rocky heights. The vantage point might reveal something, anything, a glimmer of hope that would lead them back to civilisation. He would find a way to get home, but as far as he was concerned, Mark could stay on the island and rot.

THIRTY FIVE

Mark stumbled back, his mind reeling from the whirlwind of memories and emotions. He felt like he was unravelling, like the threads of his existence were fraying at the edges. He looked down at the boy, his younger self, whose brown eyes were a mirror to his own confusion and fear.

"You're not real," he said, reaching up to his face to rub his eyes.

As he moved his arm, he couldn't help seeing the blister on his hand. It was a garish red. The pain was ripping through his flesh, but the size of the wound seemed unchanged. Whatever it was, at least it wasn't spreading.

"None of this is real."

Crash-landing on a tropical island was almost as unlikely to be real as being confronted by a junior version of himself. Nothing made sense to Mark. He could feel the fragile grip on his sanity slipping.

He reached into his pocket for the water bottle, suddenly unshakeably aware that his mouth was parched. When had he last drunk? Whenever it was, he had emptied the last of his reserves. The bottle was empty.

Wide-eyed and brimming with curiosity, the boy observed Mark's torment.

"Go away," Mark snapped, his voice tinged with frustration. "Why don't you just leave me alone?"

The echoes of haunting laughter and memories he'd long buried still reverberated in his thoughts.

"Go away!" Mark yelled.

He swatted his hand out towards his younger self, and the boy stood in silence, regarding him with a cold, emotionless stare.

"Go away!"

Mark lunged again, but beneath him, the ground shifted like quicksand. He tumbled forward and collided with the earth with a heavy thud. Darkness encroached on his consciousness, and as it did, he heard those two words, haunting and relentless.

"End it."

The passage of time remained elusive as Mark

drifted in and out of consciousness. Gradually, the jungle came into focus, but the playground, swings, and his younger self were gone. A peculiar blend of relief and disappointment washed over him.

"I should have told you," he muttered, self-reproach and confusion clouding his thoughts. "But what could I have said?"

For the second time that day, Mark pulled himself from the leaf-strewn floor, up to his feet again.

"Mark?" he shouted, feeling the sense of the bizarre as he called his own name. "Are you there?"

There was no reply. The only sounds amongst the trees were the building whispers of the wind, which appeared to have picked up since he was out, and the usual calls of the native wildlife. If there ever had been a boy, he was gone.

The cryptic message from his younger self, the distorted memories of his past, all left him in a state of confusion. Even though he had regained consciousness, the world around him remained a shifting, dreamlike landscape, echoing with the remnants of his memories.

"Mark…" Mark said again, his voice rough as bark.

He needed water, and a nagging thought reverberated around his conscience. He didn't just need water to quench his growing thirst, but also to wash away the sticky residue of the strange sap from his skin. He had done his best, but hallucinating about childhood playtime wasn't quite normal. He was lucid enough to recognise that something very, very strange was happening to him.

With no further sign of the young boy, and no response to his calls, Mark had no option but to leave. He had to make his way to the stream; it was the only source of salvation he could think of.

As he walked, memories of Lucy, his childhood friend, resurfaced, like old wounds opening anew. They had once been inseparable, partners in adventure and confidants in mischief. Where had it all gone wrong?

"Not now," he told himself. "Don't think about her now."

The jungle appeared to be enclosing around him, a living manifestation of his own choices and their outcomes. His thirst grew stronger with every step he took, and dehydration was on the verge of overwhelming him. Yet, he pressed on, determined to find the stream, to wash away the sap, and to quench the unquenchable thirst that had plagued him for so long.

The heart of this unforgiving jungle was not only a battle with nature but also with the demons of his past, and the feeling that his existence hung in the balance was impossible to escape.

THIRTY-SIX

Although they hadn't seemed to walk far before stopping to answer the call of their bodily functions, the path back to the cave had stretched to miles as Emily ran, heart pounding, oblivious to any danger that might lurk nearby. She gripped the stick that had proven no use in preventing the disastrous situation, but with adrenaline pumping at an all-time high, Emily could have outrun even the fastest of beasts.

Before the intern could reach the camp, Karen came racing through the trees towards her.

"We heard shouting," she panted. "What's happened?" Looking over the intern's shoulder, it was impossible for Karen not to notice the HR manager's absence. "It's Sarah, isn't it? Where is she?"

The look on Emily's face reflected both guilt and anxious concern.

"I don't know," Emily breathed.

"Don't know?" Karen's face fell. "How can you not know?"

Emily, breathless and on the verge of tears, stammered out her reply. "I – I don't know. We..."

Karen's expression softened, but only slightly.

"Come," Karen said, draping her arm around Emily's shoulder in a way that felt more like guidance than comfort. "Come and tell us all what happened."

As they moved back towards the camp, Karen turned to take one more look behind them into the jungle. There was no sign of the brash HR manager.

When the two women broke through the trees to the camp, Michael and Liam were on their feet. The air buzzed with tension as Chen stepped forward.

"Where is she? Where's Sarah?"

Emily's breath came in short, shallow gasps. She pointed back toward the dense foliage behind her, her voice barely above a whisper. "She's gone."

"What do you mean, she's gone?" Liam asked, his voice firm but filled with unease.

Emily's eyes were wide with fear, and her words spilled out in a rush. "I stood away while she took her toilet break." Her cheeks reddened as she continued. "Then, while she went behind a tree, I thought I should take the opportunity to, er, relieve myself too, so I…well, you know. It wasn't like I was going to stare at her anyway. I stepped away for a minute, that's all. Just a minute. When I came back, she was gone. I called for her, but there was no answer. I looked around, but I couldn't find her anywhere."

The news hung in the air like a heavy fog. Liam exchanged a glance with Chen, both realising the gravity of the situation. Ryan Bellamy had been sitting on a log nearby, listening to their conversation intently. He stood up, his face paling.

"It's not your fault, Emily."

A murmur between the rest of the group came in agreement.

"Don't blame yourself," Karen said. "She would have only been snotty with you if you had insisted that you kept eyes on."

Chen shot a sharp look at the software engineer. "Karen. Now isn't the time to be bitchy. Our colleague could be in danger."

"Could be? I'd say she must be. She wouldn't have walked off on her own. She's hardly Thompson," Liam said.

"We have to go look for her," Michael said, taking charge of the situation. "Emily, can you show us where you last saw her? Liam and I can find her. You two come back here and stay with Bellamy."

"Stay here because we are women and somehow that makes us fragile and incapable of being useful in the jungle?" Karen shot, with barbed words.

"Sarah has already gone missing," Chen said, his calm voice only irritating Karen further.

"Someone has to be here when Jackson comes back," Bellamy reasoned. "And if Mark does."

The mention of Thompson's name seemed to soften Karen's anger.

The team of seven that had set off on the trip to Azure Haven had dwindled to only four. Jackson would return, and Karen was sure that Mark would, too. But Sarah? Was she really the type to do something as foolish as wander off in the jungle alone? For all the antagonism between them, the thought of the HR manager coming to any harm out there was terrifying.

"Okay," Karen said in quiet acceptance.

Emily nodded rapidly.

"We'll go together to where you last saw her, and then, Ryan, you bring the girls back here."

Karen was too exhausted to complain about Chen's use of the pejorative word. There were more serious problems to combat.

The dense foliage closed in around Emily, and the

team she led as they followed the winding path that led to the spot where she had last seen Sarah. The forest seemed to hold its breath, the oppressive humidity making every step feel like a monumental effort.

As they approached the rest stop, Emily came to a standstill.

Her voice trembled as she recounted the events. "We were here, just a few minutes ago. Sarah and me. She went over that way," Emily pointed. "I stayed here, and then, uh, I went behind that tree."

"Did you see how far into the bushes she went?" Chen asked.

Emily shook her head. "Far enough to be out of sight. I thought it was okay, though. She deserved some privacy, right?"

"No one is blaming you," Bellamy calmed. "We just need to narrow the search area for the boys."

Karen flicked her eyes towards Bellamy, wondering if he had used the word purposely. There was no sign of recognition on his face.

Chen had already stepped away in the direction that Emily had showed them. In the distance, he was crouching to examine the ground, his analytical mind racing to make sense of the situation. Among the leaves and twigs, he noticed a faint trail of broken branches and disturbed foliage leading deeper into the jungle.

"Look at this," Chen said, his voice steady despite the growing unease. "It seems like she headed in that direction." He pointed to the path marked by the disturbed vegetation.

Liam nodded, his apprehension mirrored in his eyes.

"Let's follow it. Maybe she left a clue farther down. We must be able to find some trace of her this way."

Although he didn't know what he would do if he needed to use it, the sturdy stick in his hand felt reassuring.

Bellamy patted the IT expert on the back.

"Go find her," he said. Turning to Chen, he continued, "And be careful, guys."

Both Liam and Michael gave terse smiles and then faced each other with stoic determination before pressing on into the jungle where Sarah had last been seen.

Ryan and the two women turned, frustrated and afraid, back to the camp.

THIRTY-SEVEN

Jonathan Jackson wiped the sweat from his brow, his fingers trembling as he clutched his empty water bottle. The unforgiving sun beat down on the dense jungle around him, turning the air into a simmering cauldron. He'd been walking for hours, a mix of anger, hatred, and longing fuelling his every step.

The memories of the office, of Thompson's smug face, came rushing back. Jackson had been on the verge of truly making his mark, the culmination of years of hard work. But then Thompson, with his conniving charm, had screwed everything up for him. Now Jackson had nothing but a bitter taste of betrayal and a burning desire for revenge. With every step, the taste became more acidic, and the fire became more powerful.

If only Thornicroft could see us now.

Jackson smiled wryly at the thought, though there was nothing pleasing about it.

When Jackson finally made his way back to the stream, he showed no restraint. He slung the bag from his shoulder onto the ground without thinking. Then, fully clothed, still wearing his dishevelled suit trousers and the T-shirt he had reluctantly accepted from Thompson's case, now sweat-stained and dappled with dirt, he threw himself into the shallow flowing water. The chill of the stream flowed over him as he lay in its path. He splashed like an infant in a bathtub, rejoicing in the feel of the soothing cold.

Turning, he pressed his face into the flow. Reddened by the day's sun, streaked with salty mud splatters, the immersion brought exquisite release. Clean and cooled, he opened his mouth and let the flowing water fill his mouth. He drank greedily and without restriction. For the briefest moment, the stream consumed his every thought. Mark, the island, and even Helena swam from his mind as it was flooded by the physical relief he finally felt.

Jackson let out a long sigh, and lay on his back, still in the current.

A sudden thought made him snap upward, leaping out of the water like a salmon.

No.

His wallet.

No.

His heart raced as he retrieved the wallet, its leather now soaked through, heavy and limp in his trembling hand. The photograph inside, the cherished image of him and Helena, clung to the leather with the tenacity of memory.

"No!" he exclaimed aloud.

The image of him and Helena had adhered firmly.

No. Please, no.

He pulled gingerly at the corner of the print, but even with the smallest amount of pressure, the paper came apart in his hand. He withdrew his fingers to find a swirl of colours on the scrap of photograph that had separated from the rest of the picture.

"No!" he hollered. "No!"

He had acted rashly, acted on his instincts, and he had lost the only thing on the island that he cared about. The picture from Florence was ruined, beyond repair. And Jackson had no one to blame but himself.

With a heavy heart and a sense of profound loss, Jackson pushed himself to his feet. The weight of his mistake pressed down on him, a crushing reminder of his impulsive actions. He had lost something irreplaceable. Tears welled in his eyes, mingling with the fresh stream water on his face, a bitter mixture of anguish and regret. He had lost Helena. If he never escaped the island, he would never see her face again.

His clothes clung to his body, the wet fabric a reminder of his stupidity.

The carryall sat accusingly beside the stream. He knew that within it he held the means to provide water to his team: the bottles, the condoms that he had planned to use as water skins. Jackson looked at the zipped black bag for seconds that felt like stretched hours.

There were two options. Take the water back to his InnovaTech colleagues or press on, ascend the vantage point and survey for a way off the island.

I can stop for their water on the way back.

Jackson turned his head, looking for signs of the raised ground. The trees were densely packed. If he hadn't found the map, he wouldn't know that the rocky heights existed.

It's a sign. I have to do this.

He took his own water bottle and filled it.

I have to find a way back home.

He left the holdall beside the stream, and turned away, in the direction indicated on the found map.

I have to get back to Helena.

THIRTY-EIGHT

As they walked, searching for clues, Chen and Liam exchanged glances, their unease mounting with each step. They called out Sarah's name repeatedly, their voices tinged with desperation, but the only response was the eerie echo of their own calls.

Liam's eyes darted around nervously, the humid air pressing in on him like a heavy weight. Sweat beaded on his forehead, despite the coolness of the jungle's shade.

"Do you really think we're going to find her?"

Chen shot a reproachful look.

"Of course," he said. "We have to believe that we will."

"I don't know what I believe after the day we've had," Liam said.

Chen looked at Liam with a considered expression, as if trying to work out what the other man was thinking.

"It's been…unusual," he said, in a measured tone.

"Jackson and Thompson leap into their leader roles, finding the plane, searching for water…" Liam pouted.

"Storming off in a huff," Chen smiled.

"If either of us had walked away from the camp, I'm sure no one would have even noticed," Liam said.

"Don't be ridiculous," Chen replied. "There are only seven of us." He couldn't count Sarah as truly lost. Not yet.

"Come on, you must feel it too," Liam said.

"It?" Chen asked. "What is this '*it*' that you think I feel?"

"We're caught up in this, but we aren't really part of it. It's Mark and Jonny's fault that we're here, and now they've got us into this mess, they are off doing the heroic or stupid shit, and we…well, what exactly are we here for?"

Chen stopped dead in his tracks, forcing Liam to backtrack a couple of paces to come back alongside.

"I don't know about you," he said. "But there are more important things I could be doing. I have other work to do back at the office. I never wanted to be a part of a foolish team-building getaway. I'm not even part of a team. I run my department, and that department consists of me."

"Same," Liam said, nodding. "I don't want to cause any bad blood here, mate, but I don't see any of you unless you have a problem. The only time anyone comes downstairs is when they need something. There's no 'would you like a cuppa, Liam?' or 'we've got drinks after work, are you in?'. Jackson doesn't even remember my name."

The resentment simmered in the humid air as they walked.

"Perhaps that's why we're here," Chen said, after a thoughtful pause.

"We're like NPCs. There's no reason at all for us to be part of this. We're just filler." Liam explained his thoughts the best he could.

Chen shook his head. "What would happen if you or I ceased to exist?"

"Jeez, man. I don't know. I've already survived a plane crash today, but I'm still not too confident about my chances." Liam managed to laugh as he spoke.

"At the office, I mean. As part of InnovaTech."

"I don't know about you, but the first time one of those dumbasses can't work out how to install their software updates or reset the password that they've probably got written on a pretty pink Paper Crane post-it on their desk…they'd be screwed."

Liam's expression reflected a change in his thinking.

"Exactly. And without me, they'd be stumbling in the dark."

"This is going to sound ironic under the circumstances," Liam said, "But I'm not sure I know what you do."

"Mostly research," Chen said. "And then some analysis."

Liam tilted his head. "Hilarious."

"I do everything, really," Chen sighed. "Keep my eye on the market, look for opportunities, work out risks and benefits."

Liam was already looking away.

"I know. It's dull to you, but I spent ten years studying to be where I am now. You wouldn't notice what I do unless I wasn't there."

"Well, Toto, I'm sorry to remind you, but we really aren't in InnovaTech anymore."

The two men shared a look. Talk of their office roles and mutual feelings of exclusion had lifted a burden from them, but that couldn't help them in their current predicament. On the island, specialist skills counted for nothing unless they were those that could help the team survive and find a means of escape.

"I haven't seen any clues to Sarah's whereabouts for a while," Liam said grimly. "You?"

Chen shook his head. There had been no more

footprints, no broken branches, no sign of her at all. Although the men called her name, Sarah had not responded. Listening to the sounds of the jungle, neither of them could hear distress cries. It was as though the undergrowth had opened up and swallowed their colleague.

With each step, their hope of finding Sarah dwindled. The jungle seemed to absorb their cries, muffling their calls for help. They were adrift in a sea of emerald foliage. Bonded by their own isolation, Chen and Liam had each other, but Sarah, somewhere out there, was alone.

THIRTY-NINE

Mark was sure he had memorised the path to the stream. Setting off straight on into the jungle from the beach, they had turned right a few hundred meters in, following the path of least resistance through the dense growth. Jackson had ducked beneath a low branch; Thompson had leap-frogged over it. Being more agile than the old man, Mark could make moves that his colleague must have abandoned twenty years in the past.

But the mental map that Mark had created had the beach as his starting point, and he didn't have a compass to orientate himself to his new position on the island. His mind was swimming as it was, without trying to align the snapshot he had memorised with his current location. He would have to either get back to the beach where they had started, or head out into the depths of the jungle, hoping he would meet the stream.

The world swayed before him. Whatever had caused him to see the fragments of his past seemed less intense now, but Mark still felt as though he had drunk three vodkas too many. There was a taste of copper with a sour acidic undertone in his dry mouth. Even in his dazed state, a shot of vodka would have been welcomed.

Shaking his water bottle brought the droplets together, but when he put it to his mouth, there was only enough fluid to wet his lips.

If there was something he needed to end, it would have to wait. Far be it for Mark to ignore the command of a trippy hallucination of his young self – for he had convinced himself that this was the only viable explanation – but he needed water, or the only thing that would be ended was his life.

Standing in the humid haze of the faltering afternoon, Mark considered his next move.

"Afternoon," he thought. "So, the sun is…" Mark peered through the canopy of trees. The glow of sunlight was coming from his left. "West? North? West. Of course, it's heading west."

Shaking his head, Mark realised it didn't matter what direction the sun was in, if he had no compass or any idea of the bearing that would take him to the stream.

"Shit," he muttered. He had to get moving. But which way?

Think, Mark. Think.

When they had turned from the beach that morning, the sun had been on his right. It was hardly an accurate means of locating the coordinates of the water he so desperately needed, but he needed it so desperately that he knew he had to take the shot. He faced away from the sun and began to walk.

Each of Mark's staggered steps forward felt like trudging through treacle. His limbs were heavy and aching. A small voice inside his head told him he should never have left the group, but Mark was an expert at blocking out the words he did not want to hear.

The trees were more tightly packed the further he walked into the woodland. Roots jutted out from the soil, threatening to trip him, and slowing his progress. His footsteps were uneven, faltering. Mark's body felt alien, heavy and slow, as if he were wading through a quagmire. Every step was a battle against gravity and confusion, his thoughts a tangled web of anxiety and disorientation.

The blister on Mark's hand throbbed with each heartbeat. He could still feel the sticky sap from the tree that had scratched him, traces of its resin clinging to his skin like a malevolent curse. It had been an agonising, fevered haze since that encounter, and Mark no longer felt he could trust his own mind.

Mark's first thought, when he heard the voice, was that the hallucinations had returned. The second was that it wasn't a voice at all, but that the short, sharp yelp he had taken for a *"no"* was the barking of a tropical dog.

What he knew about the flora and fauna of tropical islands was limited to coconuts and palm trees, but he had left those behind at the shoreline.

Mark stopped in his tracks, first afraid, and then intent on listening for further information to help him work out what or who was calling out, and whether he needed to find them or flee.

"No!" the voice sounded out again. It was clear, even through the muggy haze of the jungle air. It was a man's voice, raw with desperation.

There was no mistaking the whining tone. It was Jackson.

Mark rested his trembling hands on his thighs and leaned forward, thinking, thinking, thinking.

What was Jackson doing out here? Was he in trouble?

A surge of conflicting emotions washed over him. Part of him wanted to rush forward, to find Jackson and see what had driven him to cry out in anguish. But another part, a self-preserving instinct, told him to hang back, to remain unseen.

Mark crouched amidst the thick trees, his breath held, his eyes fixed on the direction of the voice.

He watched as Jackson came into view, his dishevelled figure stumbling near the stream. The man's shoulders were hunched, his posture one of defeat.

Mark's curiosity battled with his fear as he observed Jackson. The man clutched something in his trembling hand, something Mark couldn't quite make out from this distance. Then, as if in a moment of vulnerability, Jackson's shoulders heaved, and he brought the object to his face.

It was a photograph. Mark recognised it instantly. The photograph that had been in Jackson's wallet at the airfield: Helena, Jackson's wife.

Mark watched, hidden in the shadows, as Jackson gazed at the image, tears streaming down his dirt-streaked face. The sight was both heart-wrenching and strangely intimate. For a moment, Mark forgot about his own thirst, his own predicament. He felt a pang of empathy for his colleague, a flicker of understanding about the things that truly mattered in life, far away from the corporate rat race they'd left behind.

But then Jackson's actions shattered that fragile connection. Mark watched as his rival got out of the stream, leaving behind the bag of water bottles that should have contained vital hydration for the team. Instead, he filled only his own bottle, as if driven by some newfound selfishness.

Mark's brow furrowed as he realised what was happening. Jackson was slipping into a survival mode of his own, a mode that left no room for teamwork or compassion. In this unforgiving jungle, it was every man for himself.

As he watched Jackson walk away, Mark's earlier empathy turned to a steely resolve. He couldn't rely on his colleague for help or guidance. None of the team could.

FORTY

The campsite was bathed in the relentless heat of the afternoon sun, and the air hung heavy with tension. Emily sat on a fallen log, her expression one of quiet concern as she surveyed their surroundings. Karen paced back and forth like a caged animal, her frustration palpable. Her footsteps created erratic patterns in the dirt, mirroring the turmoil in her mind. She could feel the weight of their predicament pressing down on her shoulders, and it was becoming too much to bear.

Emily finally broke the silence, her voice calm but tinged with weariness. "Karen, you're wasting your energy. You should sit for a while."

Karen's head snapped towards Emily, her eyes blazing with a mixture of anger and desperation.

"And what exactly are you doing, Emily? Huh? Sitting there staring into the jungle won't change a damn thing!"

Emily sighed, the tension in the air thickening.

"I didn't mean it like that. We're all worried, but pacing won't make them come back any faster."

Karen's shoulders slumped, her frustration turning to resignation.

"I just can't stand this waiting. We don't even know if they're okay out there. And Sarah…"

Her voice trailed off, and the mention of Sarah's name hung between them like a heavy, unspoken truth. One woman felt the responsibility of Sarah's disappearance on her watch, the other bore the memory of the fight that had taken place between them only hours earlier.

"It's okay," Emily said. "I know you're not exactly the best of friends. You can still be concerned about her."

Karen nodded, her eyes glistening with tears.

"I never meant to…I mean, what if she left of her own accord too? First Mark, and then Sarah? No one can bear to be around me. They would rather take their chances in the jungle than be here with me."

Her voice broke as she finished the sentence, and Emily rose to her feet and hurried to Karen's side, wrapping her in a warm embrace.

Karen's pent-up tears turned into sobs, and she pressed her head against Emily's shoulder as she released the emotion that had been building for far longer than the time they had spent on the island.

Bellamy, hovering by the cave, turned his eyes away and let the women have their moment.

"I'm sorry," Karen stammered.

Emily merely shook her head and tightened her hold on her colleague. The jungle had stripped away their comforts, exposing their vulnerabilities in the most unforgiving way. It didn't have to strip them of their humanity, too.

When Karen finally stepped back, she mopped at her tears with the bottom of her T-shirt.

"Mark's T-shirt," she said as she dabbed at her eyes. Her voice was on the verge of breaking again.

Emily put her arm out and rested it on Karen's shoulder, trying to extend the reassurance.

"Karen," she said. "What happened between you two? I mean, if you don't want to…"

Karen shook her head and gestured towards the log.

"Let's sit down. No need for us to both waste our energy," she said with a smile that looked like it took a lot of effort to make.

Emily rested back on the log, and Karen sat beside her. Flicking her eyes over to Bellamy, Emily saw him give her a thumbs up gesture, before turning and sitting in the cave's mouth, presumably out of earshot.

Karen hesitated for a moment, the internal struggle evident in her eyes. Finally, she spoke, her voice laced with regret and sadness.

"I've never talked to anyone about this before. I don't have many friends outside of work." Karen paused again and let out a sigh before adding, "Or at work."

Emily gave an understanding nod.

Karen took a deep breath.

"You have to know that I had been separated from my husband for ten months. We were about to finalise our divorce. He left me for someone else."

Emily nodded again, silently urging Karen to continue.

"I was on my own all that time. You could say I was alone even longer. Before I found out about the other woman, the distance was…immense. I think I had been alone for years."

She looked up at Emily for acknowledgement before continuing.

"One night, Mark and I were working late at the office. It had been a particularly long and gruelling day. Another tight deadline for a project that took much longer than we had bargained for. It must have been ten o'clock before we finished. Neither of us had managed to get dinner. I was exhausted, emotionally drained and, well, pretty damn lonely."

Karen's voice wavered as she recalled the memories. "We decided to grab a drink, unwind a bit. But… one thing led to another, and we started seeing each other."

Emily listened attentively, her face a canvas of understanding. There was no need to spill the details. This wasn't the InnovaTech water fountain, this was a vulnerable shared moment at a time of crisis.

As she relived the past, Karen gazed out into the jungle.

"Mark… he was emotionally absent, always keeping his distance. He said we probably shouldn't have a relationship because of work." She shook her head, as if still reeling from the let-down. "I thought it was just an excuse."

Tears welled up in Karen's eyes once more, and she blinked them back. "He pretended he never felt anything for me, like it was all a mistake. But I… I thought we could have had something special."

Emily reached out and placed a comforting hand on Karen's shoulder.

"I blame myself for everything that's gone wrong, not just in my life, but… here, on this damn island."

"Karen, you can't blame yourself, you just can't. Relationships are complicated, and sometimes they just don't work out. And this island? That's nuts. Nothing that has happened has been your fault."

Karen nodded, but the weight of her past choices still hung heavily.

"Maybe he didn't want me because I have kids; he didn't want the complication. Maybe it's because I'm just not enough."

Emily squeezed Karen's shoulder gently. "You are more than enough, Karen. Don't ever doubt that."

"I'm a software engineer," she said, looking up through a veil of tears. "Look at you. You must be five years younger than I am. Maybe more. I've been in the same job since I left university. I work every hour I can just so I can put food on the table for my kids," Karen said. "You can't understand because you don't *have* kids. You don't have the stress of finding childcare, paying for that childcare in a single income, because do you think my ex-husband gives me a penny?"

Emily's eyes were filled with sympathy.

"No," Karen continued, answering her own question. "I get nothing from him. And when the times come around that I want more than anything to be with my kids – birthdays, Christmas – they want to be with their dad because they don't get to see him any other time. I swear he literally uses those days against me. The days I've worked all year for. Do you not think I would rather be taking them to school, bringing them home, spending evenings with them instead of leaving the office just in time to kiss them goodnight?"

"It sounds like you've been having a shitty time," Emily said in a soft, calming voice.

"Mark was…" Karen looked out in the direction that her former lover had walked. "He wasn't just a distraction for me. He made me feel alive again. At first, anyway. He made me feel like I could find the smile that I hadn't been able to wear for…" She shook her head. "For so, so long."

"I can't speak for him, Karen. I don't know how he feels, but I think…I think he has some issues of his own he needs to work through. There's nothing wrong with you. Nothing at all."

"There's something wrong with all of us," Karen replied with a sharp laugh. "This whole shitshow is like *The Wizard of Oz*. Thornicroft is the man behind the curtain, while we all stumble around in the jungle trying to find the yellow brick road so we can get back home again. Mark doesn't have a heart; you certainly didn't seem to have any courage before today. Sarah…"

Rather than comparing Sarah to the brainless scarecrow, thinking of her name again brought Karen back to the present moment and the predicament they were in.

"I don't know what I'm doing in the office yet," Emily confided. "There's so much to learn, and I'm trying so hard, but…"

"We all treat you like crap and expect you to know as much as we do, even though you've only been with us for two months. Yeah, I know," Karen said, shamefaced.

"I do know some things about survival, though," Emily smiled. "At work and in the wild."

"So, I've noticed," Karen said.

"Wild camping with my dad," Emily explained, but there was a sadness in the way she spoke.

Karen thought better than to open further emotional wounds. They *were* wasting their energy; their mental strength was almost exhausted.

"Listen," Karen said. "I know we said we would stay here and wait for Liam and the doctor, but… they've been gone so long. We need water, and soon we're going to need food too. Either you and I can go together, with Bellamy here waiting for the others, or the three of us can set out as a group. We have to get to the stream or find water somewhere else. I trust you, Emily. I know you can help me."

The expression of happiness on the intern's face seemed woefully out of place under the circumstances, but she couldn't conceal the pride that arose from hearing Karen's words.

"I can help us," she said. "Let's ask Bellamy what he thinks and take it from there."

Karen nodded in earnest.

With a shared determination, they walked across to Bellamy.

FORTY-ONE

As Jackson traced the route of the stream towards the high ground, the world around him began to fade, replaced by the internal echoes of his past. His mind was a tempest, with swirling thoughts of his hatred for Mark set against those of love for Helena. The sweltering heat, oppressive and unforgiving, clung to his skin, while the cacophonous buzz of insects provided a dissonant soundtrack for his journey.

The sun was beginning to fall, which meant two things: his teammates would need the water that he had not yet gathered for them, and he had to hurry if he was to make it to the top of the outlook before sunset and be back at the camp before dark. Trying to make his way through the jungle at night was a surefire way to get himself killed. If he didn't fall on the precarious terrain, he would surely be stalked by a hungry beast.

The clock was ticking. He had to hurry.

I have to get home to you.

Every step was a searing reminder of his anger, his frustration, his burning need to prove himself. He climbed the steep incline of the rocky peak with single-minded determination, each foothold a challenge to the forces that had conspired against him.

How could I have been so stupid?

As he ascended, the surrounding jungle closed in, a living, breathing entity. The thick canopy above cast dappled shadows on the narrow path, a dance of light and darkness that mirrored the turmoil in Jackson's mind. His footsteps grew heavy, sweat pouring down his face in rivulets, mixing with dirt and grime. He couldn't afford to stop now; he was on a mission driven by loathing and a desperate need to escape.

The photograph. Helena.

Although Jackson tried to focus on the image of his wife's face, the more he thought, the more he realised. There had been an insurmountable distance between them for longer than he cared to admit. It wasn't this island that had put space between them; it had been him. Always him.

"I messed up," he whispered to the winds that

gently tugged at his clothes as he forged onwards.

Helena, her radiant smile, and infectious laugh, how they had danced around the idea of starting a family. Every "not now" and "maybe later" felt like a dagger to his heart, each recollection piercing deeper than the last. And then, when he finally agreed to try, there was nothing. The child Helena had longed for, waited patiently for, never came.

It had been the endless meetings, the corporate events, the drive to climb the professional ladder that had consumed him. He had rationalised each decision, each moment away from home. But now, with the endless expanse of time and the solitude of the wilderness, those rationalisations seemed so trivial. The weight of his regrets bore down on him as he walked on.

As he trekked further up, the babbling stream grew louder, its flow more robust and hurried. He stopped momentarily, placing his hand on a moss-covered rock, feeling its coolness. He splashed some of the water onto his face, hoping it would wash away the guilt, but it only amplified his reflections.

He had only wanted to succeed. He had only wanted to be the best.

He wanted to be the one to secure the Tursten Mitchell account. If Mark had offered to read over the proposal or check the email before he sent it, he knew in his heart that he would have refused.

He would have clicked the send button with arrogance and sent his error to the prospective client all the same.

He wanted to be the one to reach the high ground and find a way off the island. If Mark had offered to work with him, to map the island as a team or search together for an escape, he knew just as surely that he would have declined the offer.

Recognition was the prize that he had always sought. He had committed his time to his work rather than his wife, and now he was lost and alone. He had nothing. He had no one.

His thoughts circled like vultures overhead, tearing at his resolve. Should he have brought water for the others? Guilt gnawed at him, but he pushed it away. If he could find a way off this forsaken island, they would all be saved.

With renewed determination, Jackson continued his climb, driven by the hope of finding a vantage point. The hope of being the hero.

The summit loomed above, a jagged crown against the relentless blue sky. Jackson's heart pounded in his chest as he neared the top. He needed to see, to find a way out, a path back to the life he had left behind. The climb grew steeper, the incline unforgiving, but he pushed himself harder, driven by the need to escape this place and the thoughts that threatened to possess him.

With one final surge of energy, Jackson reached

the peak. At the top of the incline was a wide, flat summit. Grey rock, speckled with shreds of life, clumps of grass and ferns fighting to survive on the barren wind-whipped land.

I made it. I made it, Helena.

The world spread out before him, a vast expanse of jungle and sea. He was high above, the entirety of the island sprawled out below him. From this vantage, he could see the distant shoreline, the thick canopy of trees, and the cave where the rest of the crew was likely still waiting.

He felt both minuscule and overwhelmingly significant in the grand scheme of things. From up here, the world seemed both vast and confined, a reflection of the paradox he felt inside.

But no matter which direction he looked, there was no sign of civilisation, no glimpse of rescue. Only the harsh reality of the island's isolation.

The island was a labyrinth, a maze with no way out. He had risked everything for nothing, just like in his work life. The realisation hit him like a physical blow. He sank to his knees, the weight of his actions pressing down on him. His hatred for Mark, his yearning for Helena, the regret for the life he had forsaken—all of it bore down on him. His tears mingled with the sweat on his face, and he knew he was truly alone, trapped not just on this island, but within the confines of his own choices.

"I'm sorry," he cried. "I'm sorry!"

The wind took his words and scattered them,

never to be heard.

He had made it to the summit, but it was a victory that tasted of ashes.

FORTY-TWO

Mark waited in the shelter of the trees until Jackson continued his journey. When he was sure his colleague had moved on, he staggered to the stream like a parched traveller who'd stumbled upon an oasis in a merciless desert. His thirst had evolved into a maddening sensation, a dryness that seemed to extend from his tongue down to his very soul.

The pain in his head throbbed, a merciless reminder of his ordeal. The blister on his hand, angry and red against his sun-kissed skin, stung, and he plunged it into the shallow water.

As he cupped the stream's offerings in his hands, Mark brought the water to his parched lips. It was like liquid salvation, filling his mouth with the sweet taste of life. The chill flowed down his throat, rejuvenating his body and mind. He allowed himself a few more gulps, savouring the sensation before bending down to wash his face.

The sap had left a residue that seemed to cling to his skin, a constant reminder of his earlier hallucinations and the phantom image of his younger self. He rubbed his scalp vigorously, trying to remove every last trace of the sap, feeling the familiar texture of his hair beneath his fingers.

Even if he could wash away the sap, he couldn't erase the memory of the visions it had caused him to see.

What the hell was that all about?

His memories of the hallucinations were like fragments of a dream, but one image remained vivid: Lucy, his childhood friend. They had been inseparable as kids, exploring the woods behind their houses, sharing secrets, and laughing until their bellies ached. But as they grew older, Mark's relentless drive to outdo everyone, including Lucy, had strained their friendship until it snapped, and they drifted apart.

He dipped his hands into the cool, clear water, once more hissing as he scrubbed the sticky residue from his skin, the memory of Lucy's distant gaze haunting him. What had she become?

Had she found happiness while he had been drowning in his competitive world, sacrificing relationships for success?

As Mark washed his face, the water's soothing touch reminded him of simpler times when life was measured in tree climbing contests and not ruthless corporate battles. The harsh truth hit him like a punch in the gut: he had lost himself, his friends, and his happiness in pursuit of being the best. And now, stranded on this forsaken island, it all seemed so meaningless.

Mark's thoughts shifted to Jonathan Jackson, the man who now seemed like his eternal rival. Jackson had abandoned their team, forsaking them without a second thought. Mark couldn't fathom how someone could be so selfish, especially in a situation like this. A flicker of anger ignited within him.

With renewed determination, Mark decided to fill the team's water bottles, a duty that Jackson had inexplicably neglected.

"I won't leave my colleagues in the lurch," he resolved. "I won't stoop to Jackson's level."

As he knelt by the stream, filling the bottles one by one, he couldn't help but wonder where Jackson was headed. His footsteps had left an indelible path, and Mark knew he had to follow. If there was one thing he couldn't tolerate, it was being outdone by Jackson.

What's he planning now?

Mark's mind raced with possibilities.

Is this another ploy to prove he's better than me?

With the bottles filled, Mark shouldered the carryall and set off along the path that Jackson had taken, his determination echoing through the dense jungle. His anger toward Jackson was palpable, but there was also a gnawing feeling of regret. Regret for letting competition blind him to the value of relationships, and for letting Lucy, his childhood friend, slip through his fingers.

The jungle closed in around him, an impenetrable wall of green that seemed to whisper his failures and regrets. He had a sinking feeling that confronting Jackson wouldn't be the end of their problems. Still, he walked.

Mark Thompson's heart pounded in his chest as he finally reached the top of the rocky incline. His breaths came in ragged gasps, a blend of exhaustion and the searing tension that had driven him to confront Jonathan Jackson. The sight that met his eyes was both desolate and unforgiving.

The barren expanse of grey rock, its surface rough and unforgiving, stretched out before him. A scattering of tenacious vegetation clung to life in the cracks and crevices, a stark contrast to the lush jungle that enveloped the island below. The sky extended above him, an endless blue canvas, but it offered no salvation, no rescue from this isolated nightmare.

Mark's eyes scanned the horizon, taking in the relentless expanse of dense foliage below. There was no indication of human presence, no hope of a rescue team in sight. Only the remnants of the plane crash, a twisted and charred skeleton smouldering in the distance, a cruel reminder of their predicament.

And then there was their campfire, a distant flicker of hope and despair combined. It was a tiny, distant beacon of warmth against the encroaching darkness of the jungle. Their camp, the cave where they had planned to take refuge, and the teammates he had left behind—all lay nestled within the heart of this unforgiving wilderness.

His gaze finally settled on Jonathan Jackson, who stood at the summit's edge, his back to Mark: an isolated figure against the vastness of their predicament. The tension that had driven Mark to follow him, to confront him, welled up inside him. He needed answers, explanations for Jackson's selfish actions. He needed to understand.

He needed to end it.

FORTY-THREE

Liam and Doctor Chen trudged through the intense jungle, their faces etched with worry. The relentless heat bore down on them, causing sweat to bead on their foreheads. They had been searching for Sarah for what felt like an eternity, their voices growing hoarse from calling out her name.

The once-promising rays of sunlight that filtered through the canopy above now seemed oppressive, casting eerie shadows on the jungle floor. Every rustle of leaves, every distant sound, made their hearts skip a beat, hoping it might be Sarah.

As time passed, hope waned, replaced by a

gnawing fear. They had covered so much ground, and there was still no sign of her. Doubt and despair threatened to overtake them.

"Do you think something took her?" Liam asked, his voice faltering.

"We could have just been walking in the wrong direction. We haven't seen any signs of her for...hours?" Chen replied, unsure of how much time had actually passed.

"It feels like hours," Liam said, with a nod of his head.

"We need to think about heading back to the camp. I need water, and I'm sure you..."

"Yes," Liam said, before the doctor could finish speaking. "Really badly, actually."

"Stand guard," Chen said. "I'm going to look around, see if I can find a way to get us something to drink. There must be a source somewhere; the plants are all doing just fine."

Liam nodded again and watched as Chen walked into the foliage to examine some of the nearby plants. Standing alone, he turned his eyes to scan the horizon, Trees, trees, and...

"What's that?" Liam murmured.

He squinted his eyes to bring the object into focus.

"Chen!" he called, starting towards the discovery. "Chen, come and see this."

"Don't go anywhere!" Michael called back, but it was too late. Liam was already walking into the undergrowth.

There, almost completely concealed by plant life, was a cave entrance. This was quite unlike the cave that they had left back at their camp, though.

This cave had a door.

"What the...?" Liam said, almost stumbling backwards in shock.

The door appeared to be made of metal of some kind, but it had been fashioned to look like the surrounding rock. If Liam and Chen had not stopped along their route, it would have remained hidden, unseen.

Liam hesitated, squinting at a carving that was etched into the door. It was a spiral, a snail's shell, and it seemed out of place in this untamed wilderness.

"Chen, you've got to see this," Liam called, his voice tinged with a mix of awe and confusion.

"I said wait!" Chen yelled in annoyance. "Why does no one ever..."

He stopped, midway through his sentence as he joined Liam.

He turned to the IT expert and locked eyes with him, both of the men sharing their surprise.

"Maybe the island isn't so deserted after all," he pondered.

"What the actual poppycrap?" Liam blurted.

Chen ran his fingers over the carving and peered at the symbol.

"Who would put this here?" He spoke the words

as though more impressed than confused.

"This? You know what it is?" Liam asked, in surprise.

"Do *you* know what this is?" Chen asked, his eyes locked on the symbol.

Liam scratched his head. "Can't say I do. Looks like a snail or shell. Maybe it's the home of some kind of huge sentient Sarah-eating snail. We should probably back up and leave the little fella alone, eh?"

"I'm fairly sure that, on the balance of probabilities, it is *not* that."

Chen grabbed Liam's arm, his mind racing, trying to think of a more rational explanation.

"I do know what the symbol is, though. It's the Fibonacci sequence. It's a mathematical pattern found in nature, in things like the spiral of a seashell or the arrangement of leaves on a stem."

Liam furrowed his brow, trying to grasp the concept. "That's why you're a doctor and I faked a degree from the University of Chester," he smiled. "Okay, it could be that...but what's it doing on a cave door?"

He paused and asked another, more significant, question.

"What's it doing on this island?"

Chen smiled, a glimmer of excitement in his eyes. "I think it's a clue, Liam. A code, maybe. Look here."

He pointed to the small keypad next to the

symbol, where numbers could be entered.

"The symbol relates to a sequence of numbers where each number is the sum of the two preceding ones. I can try them on the keypad, see if that's the code."

Liam couldn't conceal his confusion, nor how impressed he was by Chen's knowledge.

"This is some weird shit," he said. "The numbers aren't 4, 8, 15, 16, 23 and 42, are they?"

Chen frowned thoughtfully and shook his head.

"No. They're not."

Liam shrugged. The doctor was clearly not into the same television shows that he was.

With newfound determination, Chen recited the Fibonacci sequence as he punched in the numbers on the keypad. 1, 1, 2, 3, 5, 8… Each number corresponded to a press of a button, and as he reached the eighth number, there was a faint click.

The stone door, which had seemed impenetrable just moments ago, swung open slowly, revealing a passage into the cave's depth…Chen and Liam exchanged glances, a mix of trepidation and curiosity in their eyes.

What could possibly lie beyond that mysterious door, and could it hold any clues about Sarah's whereabouts?

FORTY-FOUR

Jonathan Jackson stood at the cliff's edge, his gaze fixed on the island below, a deep well of regret gnawing at him. The fading fire on the beach served as a harsh reminder of their hasty actions that morning. They had rushed in without a plan, without coordination, without thinking, and now the consequences were starkly evident.

The women had wasted time and energy building that fire, just because he had told them to. He should have thought first, about finding a better position, about building a camp. His urgency to explore, to be the first to find salvation, had driven him into the jungle. His arrogance had refused to let go of the idea that perhaps, just perhaps, they could still have landed on the Azure Haven Retreat island. That help could be a short walk away.

It was patently clear now that there was no retreat on the island. There was no help in sight.

Mark's rash decision to venture into the plane without a word of discussion was a glaring example of their dysfunctional teamwork. Jackson's relationship with Mark had always been one of competition and tension, and it had only intensified in the face of adversity. They couldn't agree on anything, couldn't communicate effectively, and it was tearing the team apart. He had entered without a plan, without an agreement of what to leave and what to retrieve. Of course, he was going to bring his own belongings. What had Jackson expected?

The divide between the two had grown too wide, poisoned by competition and resentment. There was no collaborative thinking. There never had been.

It had been Chen and Liam, the unlikely pair, who had stumbled upon the cave. The research analyst and the joker of the office had managed to achieve what the two supposed leaders couldn't.

And it had been the women, Emily, Sarah, and Karen, who had figured out how to transport the fire they had started on the beach to the safety of the cave. Even through Sarah and Karen's animosity, they had managed to work together for the benefit of their colleagues.

What had Jackson and Mark contributed, except for leaving their teammates behind, thirsty and alone?

Jackson's mind drifted back to the campsite he'd found earlier. Was whoever camped there part of a team, or had they always been alone? Was that what would become of him if he stayed on this island? Scribbling notes in his book, trying to make sense of the isolation until one day…nothing.

He had promised the team water, but in reality, he had done exactly the same as Mark. He had headed out into the jungle with only his own agenda in mind. He wanted to be the saviour. The leader that would get them off the island.

If only he'd paused, considered the needs of the team. He could have saved them all a trip to the stream, shared a sense of unity in this dire situation. But his desire to be the hero, to prove himself, to outshine Mark, had overridden his empathy.

The weight of his decision not to bring back water for his colleagues pressed heavily upon him. In a voice choked with remorse, he muttered an apology to the wind, admitting that he should have taken the water, should have put the team's survival above his own pride.

"I'm sorry," he said. "I should have brought the water. I'm so sorry."

But just as the words left his lips, Mark's voice cut through the humid air, cold and unrelenting. "Damn right you should have."

Jackson turned, startled, to see Mark standing behind him, his expression a mix of anger and disappointment. The tension between them crackled like a live wire. Jackson couldn't find the words to respond, his guilt and regret washing over him in waves. He had let them all down, and Mark was the living embodiment of that failure.

FORTY-FIVE

Mark Thompson approached the clifftop with a heavy heart, his steps measured and deliberate. The carryall containing the precious bottles of water swung heavily from his hand, a stark reminder of the burden he had taken upon himself. His resentment towards Jonathan Jackson simmered just beneath the surface, ready to erupt at any moment.

Jackson stood there, silhouetted against the harsh light of the sun, his gaze fixed on the island that had become their prison. Thompson's outrage at Jackson's failure to fetch the water for the team still burned within him. It was a testament to Jackson's constant need for competition, for outshining others, for putting himself first, even at the expense of the team's well-being.

With a sense of grim determination, Thompson let the carryall fall to the rocky ground with a thud. The bottles clattered together, a cacophony of sound that matched the chaos that had become their lives. He took a deep breath, his frustration bubbling up, and walked towards Jackson.

As he neared his rival, Thompson couldn't help but overhear Jackson's words.

"I'm sorry," he heard Jackson mutter, his voice carrying the weight of regret. "I should have brought the water. I'm so sorry."

Thompson's eyes narrowed, and a bitter retort formed on his lips.

"Damn right you should have," he snapped, his voice laced with anger and accusation. The confrontation that had been brewing between them for so long was finally coming to a head.

For a moment, the two men faced each other on the unforgiving clifftop, the island's harsh beauty serving as a backdrop to their bitter exchange. The years of rivalry, of one-upmanship, of putting their personal ambitions ahead of the team, had brought them to this moment of reckoning.

The sun beat down on them, casting long shadows across the rocky ground, as they stood there, finally confronting the demons that had driven a wedge between them.

The tension that had built up over the years between Mark Thompson and Jonathan Jackson exploded into violence as Mark charged at his nemesis. Jackson, driven by a mix of fear, frustration, and fury, dodged out of the way, his instincts taking over. He sprinted back into the centre of the rocky clearing. They were like two animals circling each other, trapped on this desolate clifftop, the bitterness between them palpable.

Mark didn't relent. He came at Jackson again, his fists clenched in anger, his heart pounding with a toxic cocktail of emotions—resentment, jealousy, and the desperate need to prove himself. Their voices rose, accusations flying like sharpened blades. Blame was heaped upon blame, and the weight of all their past conflicts bore down on them.

"You always had to be the best!" Mark yelled, landing a solid blow to Jackson's side.

"And you couldn't stand that I was!" Jackson retorted, staggering but retaliating with a fierce uppercut. "You ruined everything!" he shouted, his voice raw with anger. "All because you couldn't stand the thought of me succeeding!"

Thompson pushed back, his own anger simmering just beneath the surface. "You're delusional, Jacko. You've always been obsessed with being the best, no matter who you trample over. No matter who gets hurt along the way."

The image of Helena's face flooded Jackson's mind, further fuelling his anger.

"Helena understood I had to work. I had to put in the hours to give her the life she deserved," Jackson thought, but didn't share with his nemesis.

"You wouldn't know what that's like. The only person in your life is yourself. You're going to spend your life alone, and you damn well deserve it." Jackson spat in retaliation.

"I chose to be alone. I chose success," Mark thought. *"I chose to be alone. I let Lucy go."*

He also kept his thoughts to himself, using his anger and frustration to lunge again at his colleague.

The fight intensified, each man drawing on reserves of strength and anger they didn't know they possessed. Mark had the upper hand for a moment, his punches raining down on Jackson, who struggled to defend himself. He landed a series of blows that sent Jackson reeling towards the edge of the cliff. But Jackson was no stranger to adversity. He had faced down many challenges in his relentless pursuit of success.

For a moment, it appeared Mark had triumphed. He moved to deliver what he thought would be the decisive blow. With a surge of determination, Jackson flipped the script. He feinted to the left, then struck back with a well-placed jab that sent Mark stumbling backward. Mark teetered at the edge of the cliff, his arms windmilling as he fought to regain his balance. He failed and fell.

Desperation washed over him, and he reached out, fingers scrabbling for any purchase. His hand found a jagged edge of rock, and he clung to it with a white-knuckled grip, his heart pounding in his chest.

Jackson, his own breath ragged and body bruised, stood a few feet away, watching the perilous scene unfold. Their bitter fight had brought them to the edge, quite literally, and now Mark dangled above the abyss, his life hanging in the balance.

For a moment, neither man spoke. The weight of their actions, the consequences of their relentless rivalry, hung heavy in the air. It was a precarious situation, a blunt reminder of how their unyielding need to best one another had led them to the precipice of disaster.

As Mark clung to the edge, his strength waning, the choice before Jackson was clear. He could let go of his anger and resentment, reach out, and try to save his rival, or he could watch Mark slip into the abyss, his own hands forever stained with the consequences of their rivalry.

FORTY-SIX

Jonathan Jackson looked down at the man dangling from the ledge. Wide brown eyes stared back; a panicked plea came almost breathlessly from the younger man's chapped lips.

"Pull me up, mate."

The words took so much effort to force from Thompson's mouth that they were almost inaudible.

But Jackson heard.

The wind that had been building all day was whipping against Jackson's face. He wanted shelter. He wanted warmth. He wanted to be back at home. He could turn and walk away. No one would ever know that he had found Mark, let alone what had happened next. Mark Thompson had brought this upon himself. Not just by leaving the group, heading out on his own, trying to be the hero, not that. Mark was not his colleague; he was his enemy - and that had been Mark's own choice.

"Jackson," Mark gasped. "Please."

Jackson could feel the throbbing in his eye socket where the other man had landed a lucky blow. A slow, steady trickle of blood coursed past the side of his eye, down his cheek. He could tell the others it had been a stray branch, an accident. No need for them to know it was Mark. No need to…

"Jackson!" A woman's voice from the edge of the clearing. "What the hell is going on?"

The voice shattered Jackson's vengeful thoughts, pulling him back from the precipice of his own darkness. It was Sarah, her voice carrying across the plateau, cutting through the savage intensity of their fight.

Her words were like a splash of cold water to his face, a jarring reminder they were not savages but businessmen, colleagues who were meant to be learning how to work together. In that moment, the full weight of his actions crashed down upon him. He saw himself for what he had become in the relentless pursuit of success—a man who had lost his humility and nearly his humanity.

The realisation was a bitter pill to swallow, but

it was also a moment of clarity. In the depths of his soul, something stirred, a glimmer of the person he once was, the person he wanted to be. With newfound determination, he made a choice.

Without answering Sarah, Jackson summoned his remaining strength and extended a trembling hand towards Mark.

His voice firm and resolute, he said, "Grab my hand, Mark. I won't let you fall."

Mark, still gasping for breath and trembling with fear, reached out and grasped Jackson's offered hand. Jackson pulled Mark up with all the strength he could muster, feeling the weight of his rival in his grip. It was a struggle, but Jackson's heart was now infused with a sense of responsibility not just for his own life, but for those of his colleagues as well.

As Mark collapsed onto the solid ground, panting and shaken, Jackson stood over him, his chest heaving. The tension that had gripped the clifftop had dissipated, replaced by a sombre realisation of the consequences of their actions. The enmity that had defined their relationship for so long seemed to dissipate in that moment, replaced by a fragile truce born out of necessity and a newfound appreciation for life.

Sarah approached, her expression a mix of concern and bewilderment.

"What happened here?"

Jackson's voice was heavy with regret as he

glanced at Mark, then back at Sarah.

"We lost sight of what really matters, Sarah. We let competition blind us to the fact that we're a team. It won't happen again."

With those words, he made a silent promise to himself. He would strive to be a better leader, a better colleague, and a better person. Their struggle on the cliff had been a wake-up call, a stark reminder that success at any cost was a hollow victory. The true measure of success lay not in defeating others but in lifting them up, in working together, in finding the humanity that had been lost along the way.

FORTY-SEVEN

As the tension eased on the cliff top, Jackson explained to Sarah what had transpired, his voice tinged with a newfound humility. He admitted that their only chance at survival was to work together as a team, setting aside their differences and grievances.

Just as the gravity of this realisation began to sink in, a slow, mocking clap echoed across the summit. The survivors turned, startled, to find Pilot Bellamy emerging from the rim of the plateau, his face wearing an ironic grin.

"Congratulations," Bellamy said, his tone dripping with sarcasm. "You've all stumbled upon the most unique way of discovering the importance of teamwork."

Bellamy's words hung in the air, and the survivors exchanged bewildered glances.

"What do you mean?" Mark panted.

Bellamy stepped closer, his expression more serious now.

"This island, it was designed as a test. This is your team-building exercise."

Sarah and the two men exchanged sharp, shocked looks.

"There were clues scattered all around, hints at the importance of collaboration," Bellamy continued. "But none of you managed to put the pieces together. Instead, you all seemed determined to reach the top on your own. Literally." He gestured around the plateau.

"We were *meant* to crash here?" Sarah said, her face a mask of disbelief.

Bellamy raised his hands in a *you-got-me* expression.

"What kind of sick…" Jackson began.

"Thornicroft," Mark cut in. "He set this up? He set us up?"

Sarah's eyes widened in disbelief. "Thornicroft planned this? But why?"

Bellamy's eyes bore into each of them in turn. "Because he saw what we all saw—a group of individuals consumed by their own ambitions and rivalries. He wanted to teach you a lesson, to show you that success isn't just about reaching the top on your own, but about working together to overcome challenges."

Jackson was stunned into silence, his face showing his attempts to comprehend what he was discovering.

Sarah, who had been silent for a moment, cleared her throat and spoke up. "I… I staged my disappearance because I was frustrated with the others. I didn't trust Jackson or Thompson to lead us, and I thought maybe if I went off on my own, I could find something useful. I thought I could get us home."

Jackson nodded slowly, understanding finally dawning in his eyes. "So, we've been playing right into Thornicroft's hands. Our competitiveness, our unwillingness to cooperate—it's exactly what he expected."

Bellamy nodded again. "Exactly," he repeated. "You all seemed more interested in going it alone."

Jackson couldn't help but speak up. "Well, we had our reasons."

Sarah shot him a pointed look, her frustration evident. "Jackson, you tried to throw Mark off a cliff!"

Jackson sighed, realising the gravity of his actions. "That's not quite…but, yes, I know, I… I lost sight of everything."

Jackson exchanged a glance with Mark, the weight of their actions settling heavily on them. It was a harsh lesson, but perhaps one they needed to learn. The island, it seemed, held more than physical challenges; it offered a chance for personal growth and transformation.

"I won't let him get away with this," Mark said, with new anger in his voice. "Thornicroft can't do this to us."

Even though he knew human resources held no jurisdiction in the jungle, he looked at Sarah for support.

"He can't do this," she agreed, her voice soft.

Jackson shook his head and looked at the pilot, one question on his mind.

"How do we get out of here?"

FORTY-EIGHT

As they pushed into the cave, Liam and Michael Chen expected to fight their way through darkness. Instead, as the door opened, the inside of the cave was illuminated by man-made light so unexpected and bright that the pair of them lifted their arms to their faces in unison.

When their eyes had adjusted, the two men looked at each other in astonishment.

"What is this?" Liam said, mouth agog.

"I think it's patently obvious what this is," the analyst replied. "The real question is, 'What is it doing here?'"

"And who the hell stashed it here?" Liam added.

The room contained a hidden cache of supplies, meticulously organised, and neatly stacked against one wall. The contents included bottles of water, non-perishable food, and an array of survival gear, from first-aid kits to ropes and climbing equipment. It was as if someone had anticipated their arrival with an eerie level of foresight.

"What the frick is going on?" Liam asked, as he walked up to the nearest shelf and peered more closely at the stock. Then, his need for water overriding his curiosity, the IT expert picked up one of the stored bottles and waved it at the doctor. "Think this is safe?"

Chen shrugged. "I wouldn't like to say. Is it sealed?"

Liam nodded. His thirst too great to resist, he uncapped the bottle and drank until it was empty.

"I guess I'll find out," he said.

Chen observed his colleague's face for a few moments before grabbing a drink for himself. He took one small tentative sip. The water tasted fresh and pure. Satisfied, Chen knocked it back almost as quickly as the other man had.

"Live together, die together," he said with a wry laugh.

Along with the supplies and equipment were other treasures which the men looked upon with wide eyes. There was a range of peculiar devices adorned with intricate symbols and mysterious machines that seemed to defy explanation.

Liam picked up a bizarre contraption from the cache. It was unlike anything they had seen before, an intricate apparatus adorned with cryptic buttons and dials.

"What in the name of Chucky is this?" Liam spurted in disbelief.

Chen furrowed his brow, examining the cryptic device.

"For once, I am at a loss," he said. He let out a deep sigh. "We should take some of this back to the camp."

Liam smiled and shook his head. "No," he disagreed.

The doctor looked at him with an expression of surprise.

"And why wouldn't we?" he asked.

"Because we should bring our camp here."

Chen smiled at his coworker. "With ideas like that, I don't think we need those project alphas."

The thought of Mark and Jackson made Liam wince.

"I hope they're alright though," he said. "Wherever they are."

Chen nodded. "Look, let's do a quick stock take and then head back. It will be getting dark soon and the girls will wonder where we are."

"You know, I'm not sure they like being called 'the girls'," Liam said, not unkindly.

"You're probably right," Chen replied. "But I don't like being called 'The Chinese Doctor' and I seem to get that all the time."

Liam nodded in recognition. "We could all probably make a few changes," he smiled.

The unlikely allies began their analysis of the room's contents, making a note of anything and everything that could be of use. What they were really hoping for was a way of calling for help. What they wanted most was a way to get the team home.

"Chen!" Liam's call was almost a yelp. "Look at this!"

The doctor span around and in two strides was by Liam's side.

"What is it?" he asked, but by the time he reached the IT expert, he could see for himself what the man had found.

Liam was clutching a satellite phone; he passed it to the doctor. Its weight was a tangible reassurance in his hand. This was their lifeline, a conduit to the world they had left behind, and the solution to their harrowing ordeal.

Liam's voice broke the reverie. "Can you believe this, Chen? We've found it, the way out."

Chen nodded, his eyes gleaming with a mixture of elation and relief. "We've found it," he repeated. "It's a miracle."

With their prize in hand, they contemplated their next move. It was tempting to rush back to the group, to share the exhilarating news of their discovery and reunite with their fellow survivors. They knew it would be a moment of immense relief and joy, a turning point in their desperate situation.

Chen turned to Liam, determination etched across his face. "We should go back, share this with Emily and Karen, and use the satellite phone to call for help. We can put this nightmare behind us."

Liam agreed, feeling a profound sense of hope wash over him. "You're right, Chen. We'll tell them, and soon we'll be on our way home."

Suddenly, the joy drained from his face, the colour along with it, leaving him ashen.

"But what about Sarah?" he said.

Chen gulped noticeably, his Adam's apple rising and falling as his brain raced.

"Damn it!" he cursed. In all the excitement of their find, their missing colleague had slipped from their thoughts.

Solemnly, he took Liam's hand.

"We will find her," he said. "Or someone else can help us," he said, pointing his chin toward the phone. "It's not like we're going to leave her out here. We all get out of here together."

Liam nodded and shook Chen's hand.

"Together," he echoed.

As they prepared to depart, Liam clutching the satellite phone like a precious relic, the cave's atmosphere seemed to thicken with anticipation. Smiling at the thought of their near imminent salvation, the men walked towards the exit.

Only a couple of steps away from the door, the men stopped dead in their tracks. The door was swinging open. Chen and Liam exchanged nervous glances, Liam's fingers tightening around the satellite phone.

As the door widened, a sliver of pale light sliced through the darkness, revealing the silhouette of a figure on the other side.

FORTY-NINE

Pilot Bellamy took a deep breath, his eyes fixed on the bewildered faces of the group.

"I need to call the helicopter," he stated plainly.

The team exchanged puzzled glances.

Sarah furrowed her brow.

"Call the helicopter? But we arrived on the plane; it crashed here. You…we…"

Bellamy nodded slowly. "That's what you were made to believe. In reality, you were all drugged as soon as you boarded the plane."

"The juice?" Sarah said in astonishment.

Again Bellamy nodded. "You're getting it. We landed on another island entirely, from which you and your luggage were transported here."

Jackson's voice was heavy with disbelief. "So, we did land at Azure Haven Retreat?"

Bellamy's response was stark and unequivocal. "'Azure Haven Retreat' doesn't exist."

Pilot Bellamy's revelation hung in the humid air like a heavy shroud, casting a shadow of disbelief over the group. 'Azure Haven Retreat', the supposed paradise of corporate team building, had been nothing more than a mirage, a fabricated illusion that had lured them into this nightmarish ordeal.

As they struggled to comprehend the truth, Bellamy offered more insight into the sinister machinations behind their predicament.

"'Azure Haven Retreat'," he explained, "was a fictional construct, a name given to the idea of escape, of transformation through adversity. It was designed to test your limits, to push you beyond your comfort zones, and to force you into a crucible where teamwork would either make or break you."

He continued, his voice tinged with regret, "Richard Thornicroft, your boss, believed that your team needed a wake-up call, that your competitiveness had spiralled out of control and was jeopardising the future of InnovaTech. He saw this extreme experience as a way to bring you all back together, to remind you of the importance of collaboration and cohesion."

The group exchanged stunned glances, the weight of Thornicroft's deception sinking in. They had been pawns in a high-stakes game, manipulated into confronting their own flaws and shortcomings.

Bellamy's tone turned sombre. "I've brought countless teams to this island, and most of them have emerged stronger, more united. But for some, the challenges were too great, the rifts too deep to mend."

Jackson couldn't help but recall the gruelling moments he had spent battling the jungle's unforgiving terrain, his desperate quest to reach the summit, and the near-tragic confrontation with Mark.

Sarah couldn't contain her anger and confusion any longer. "But why? Why put us through all of this?"

Bellamy wiped his brow, his expression serious. "I work for a company that specialises in extreme team-building expeditions for elite teams that simply can't seem to work together. We're an expensive solution, but Thornicroft must have thought you were worth the investment."

Jackson's mind whirled as he remembered the journal he had discovered in the jungle. "What about that journal? Was it part of the game, or did someone else…"

Bellamy cut him off, his response cryptic. "This island holds many secrets, some left behind by previous teams, and others… well, it's best not to dwell on those."

Their journey had been a twisted odyssey, a descent into chaos and conflict orchestrated by their own boss. 'Azure Haven Retreat' had never existed, but the lessons learned on this forsaken island were painfully real.

Now, with a way off the island within reach, the group was left to grapple with the knowledge that their salvation had come at a steep price—the unravelling of their deepest fears, rivalries, and insecurities.

The weight of their situation bore down on them. But Bellamy was pragmatic, shifting their focus to the task at hand. "I left Karen and Emily down at the stream. Let's go and bring them up to speed. Then you can walk back to my base with me, where we have a satellite phone to call for the helicopter."

"And that's it?" Jackson asked in abject shock. "You call a helicopter, and we are just meant to go home and…what…? Go on with our normal routine?"

"Far from it, I'd say," Bellamy said, looking the project manager in the eye. "Far from it."

FIFTY

As Sarah, Mark, and Jackson arrived at the stream with the pilot, their weary faces bore the weight of their recent experiences. Karen and Emily, anxiously awaiting Bellamy's return, were taken aback by the sight of their colleagues emerging from the jungle with him. Their faces reflected shock and disbelief.

Mark broke the silence, his voice carrying a mix of relief and frustration. "Karen, Emily, it's a long story, but we're here now."

"Sarah?" Emily didn't know whether to reach out to her colleague or lash against her.

"I'm sorry," the human resources manager said with the weight of genuine remorse.

Emily nodded and opened her arms, inviting an embrace. "It doesn't matter," she said. "I'm just glad you're safe."

Sarah laid her head onto Emily's shoulder and let the tears of frustration, stress, and gratitude flow.

"I'm glad you're safe too," Karen whispered, resting her hand on Sarah's heaving back as she sobbed.

Jackson cleared his throat, his expression stern. "We need to talk. All of us."

He proceeded to explain the bizarre events of their time on the island, how it was a meticulously orchestrated ruse by Richard Thornicroft to test them, and how Ryan Bellamy's company had been hired to carry out this elaborate charade.

Mark added, "We've got to get to Ryan's base. He has a satellite phone there. We can use it to call for help and finally get off this island."

Karen and Emily exchanged glances, the gravity of the situation sinking in. It was a lot to process, but the presence of their colleagues and the prospect of rescue infused them with newfound determination.

"What about Chen and the IT guy?" Karen said, with concern.

"Liam," Jackson reminded her. "Where are they?"

"They went to look for Sarah," Emily said, with a fearful expression. "You didn't see them, Sarah?"

Sarah shook her head, close to another bout of tears. "I'm so sorry."

Karen put a finger to her own lips. "Shh," she said. "Don't. We will find them together. Ryan, can you help us? Are there people who can...?"

The pilot was confident in his response. "You'll all be leaving together."

Emily nodded firmly. "Let's go, then. We've wasted enough time here."

With the six of them now reunited and their goal set, they turned to follow Bellamy, moving forward together, their shared experiences on the island forging a bond they never could have expected.

Mark and Karen found themselves lagging behind the others, the weight of unspoken words hanging heavy between them. Finally, Karen broke the silence, her voice soft and filled with concern.

"Mark, I was really worried about you back there. You went off on your own, and with everything that's happened..."

Mark sighed, his gaze fixed on the ground as they walked. "I needed some space, Karen. Time to clear my head."

Karen didn't let it go. "But why would you want to be alone at a time like this? We should be sticking together."

"Don't," he said, snapping his head round towards her. "Just don't."

Karen's expression changed as a thought struck her.

"You're not alone? There's...there's someone else."

A hollow laugh that sounded more like a sigh came from Mark.

"Oh, there is. But not in the way you think." Mark hesitated, then decided to confide in her. His voice was tinged with regret as he confessed that it was because of Lucy.

"Lucy?" Karen repeated, a note of curiosity and more than a touch of jealousy in her voice.

"Yeah," Mark replied, his tone heavy with emotion. "She's someone from my past, a childhood friend. I lost touch with her because of my own competitive nature, my relentless pursuit of success."

"And you've had time to think about her while you've been on the island?" Karen asked, trying to make sense of what he was telling her.

Mark looked at the woman beside him and contemplated how much of what had happened on the island he should share with her. The two of them had shared a lot, perhaps not as much as they could have, but wasn't that down to him and his idiocy?

He took a deep breath and spoke.

He gave a bitter smile. "I've let competition and ambition rule my life. I've been so focused on winning that I've lost sight of what truly matters. Lucy cut me off. We were both kids, really, teenagers. It came to a head, finally, in high school. We both ran for class president, and I…well, I behaved terribly."

Karen reached out for his hand and gave it a reassuring squeeze, urging him to go on.

"I wanted to win, you see. I wanted it to be me." He shook his head as though trying to deny the truth. "She put her flyers up. I tore them down. She was a lovely, caring person, and I told everyone how wicked she was." He flicked his eyes towards Karen. "Some of the things I said about her…" He let the sentence trail off.

"It's in the past now," Karen said. With a faint smile, she said, "At least you got to be president."

"No!" Mark barked. "I didn't. She still won. Can you believe that? I tried to destroy her, and she still won. I lost the election, and I lost my best friend. The moment the results were announced, she walked up to me, her eyes filled with both relief and sadness. Do you know what she said to me? She said, 'Mark, we could have done great things together. I wish you could see that winning doesn't always mean tearing others down.' I'll never forget it. And what did I say?"

Karen shook her head.

"I congratulated her. And then I walked away."

Salt tears mixed with the salt sweat on Mark's face.

Karen gripped more tightly on Mark's hand. "I'm sorry, Mark. I had no idea. We all have our demons, our regrets. Maybe this ordeal is a chance for all of us to confront them and find a way to move forward."

Mark looked down at the ground, his voice barely a whisper. "I thought it was something I could bury. I thought I could leave it in the past. But now, being here on this island, it's like the past is catching up with me."

"But it is the past, Mark. No matter how painful, you can't go back and change it. All you can do is focus on the present moment...and what you want in the future."

Mark pulled up, letting the others walk further ahead, and looked at Karen.

"Do you still...want something with me?" he asked, his voice weak and uncertain.

"Let's get home and talk about it then," Karen said. "It's been a hell of a day and I never make a decision on an empty stomach."

She gave him one of the stunning smiles that had drawn him to her in the first place, and then they turned to catch up with the team, not letting go of each other's hands.

FIFTY-ONE

The team reached the cave where Ryan Bellamy's base was hidden, a sense of relief washing over them. They knew they were one step closer to escaping the island and its relentless trials. As they pushed the heavy door open, the sight of Chen and Liam inside brought a collective sigh of relief. The two groups exchanged glances, a mixture of reassurance and curiosity dancing in their eyes.

While the group of six that had made their way across the island were relieved to see the two experts, there was a look of astonishment and fear on the face of the colleagues in the cave.

Once the shadow of Bellamy at the head of the

party came into focus, his Chen's expression changed.

"You..." Chen said.

"Me," said the pilot, nodding a greeting to the analyst and the techie.

"Sarah!" Liam blurted. "You're alright. Where did you...?"

Sarah stepped forward, eager to break the silence. "Chen, Liam, you won't believe what we've been through."

Emily added, "It's been like something out of a thriller novel."

Karen nodded in agreement, her eyes briefly meeting Mark's. They were still processing their own emotions and experiences.

Jackson took charge, explaining the situation to Chen and Liam in quick, concise terms. He detailed the deceptive team-building exercise, and the plan to call for a helicopter rescue, omitting his clifftop battle with his counterpart.

Chen, ever the pragmatic thinker, absorbed the information with a calm demeanour. Liam, on the other hand, seemed both awestruck and somewhat overwhelmed by the whirlwind of revelations.

As he tried to wrap his head around the bizarre turn of events, he couldn't help but blurt out, "So, you're saying we've been duped into this whole thing?"

"It was all Thornicroft," Sarah nodded.

"The audacity!" Chen scoffed. "How does he think he's going to get away with this?"

Sarah shrugged. "That's something we are going to have to deal with when we get home," she said.

With a sigh of determination, Ryan reached for the satellite phone, his fingers dialling a number he had clearly used before. The atmosphere in the cave was taut with anticipation as the phone rang, each ring feeling like an eternity. Then, a voice crackled through the device, and a wave of relief washed over them as they realised their ordeal was coming to an end.

With his voice filled with authority, Ryan Bellamy spoke into the phone. "This is Bellamy. We're ready for extraction."

As he confirmed their location and the imminent arrival of the helicopter, the tension in the room dissipated. The weary but triumphant team knew that their extraordinary adventure had irrevocably changed them, teaching them the value of teamwork, resilience, and the importance of humility.

Now, they stood together, waiting for the sound of the helicopter blades that would signal their return to civilisation, their bond forged in the crucible of a surreal island, where they had learned that sometimes, the true path to success lay not in competition, but in collaboration.

What happened next was up to them.

Thank you for reading **The Work Retreat.**

If you have enjoyed this book, please visit Amazon, Goodreads or wherever you leave reviews. Reviews help readers to find my books and help me reach new readers.

If you're posting about this book on social media, I'm @jerowneywriter, or @jerowney on TikTok. Tag me!

For further information about me and my work, and to receive a free book, please visit my website: http://jerowney.com/about-je-rowney

Best wishes,

JE Rowney

Made in the USA
Las Vegas, NV
19 June 2024